Rapture

This is my most Recent
book.
MARiAH Sorkine
August 2024

For my Mother, Faina Sonkina
With abiding love and gratitude

Marina Sonkina

Rapture

And Other Stories

BOOKS

Cover artwork by Włodzimierz Milewski

Note for libraries: A catalogue record for this book is available from Library and Archives Canada at www.collectionscanada.gc.ca

ISBN: 978-0-9952778-2-3

MW Books
Garden Bay, BC
Canada
mwbooks.ca

10 9 8 7 6 5 4 3 2 1

Contents

Acknowledgements

I'm deeply grateful to William Gelbart who published, designed and illustrated this book. His unwavering faith enabled me to overcome hurdles and reach the finish line.

I am grateful to Judson Rosengrant for his skills in translating all but one of these stories into English. Unlike my previous collections of short stories, written in English, this time I let the winds of my native tongue blow into my sails. (The exception herein is *Rapture*, written in English.)

I owe a big thanks to Eric Leif Davin, a writer, a historian and a gracious friend who believed that no lived experience should be lost. He nudged me to write, rain or shine. Without his incentive and his proofreading, the story *Rapture* would not have seen the light of the day.

Brent and Hedy Thomson, dancers, educators, writers gave me the critical impetus I needed while the protagonist of *Return* was going through her ordeal on the stage of Omsk Drama Theater.

Finally, my gratitude goes to Barry Lugar for telling me about his many years of fishing, inadvertently giving me the inspiration for *Salmon King*.

Salmon King

1

Autumn comes almost imperceptibly to the Sunshine Coast. The sky turns somber, the lakes gradually darken, and the slow-witted firs shake their beards of lichen and shrug: "What is it to us? We will stand here just as we have always stood, be it autumn or spring or winter with its downpours." Only the slender trunks of occasional aspens, incidental guests in the low-lying areas living solitary lives alongside the glum evergreens, will quiver and shed their small heart-shaped yellow leaves and then disappear, dissolving among their shaggy hosts until spring.

On one of those still warm autumn days, I turned by mistake off the main highway onto a dirt road and got lost. The road came to an end at an estate surrounded by a dense hedge of pliant yew. I stepped out of the car. Silence. Nobody anywhere. I walked through an archway entwined with faded yet still fragrant honeysuckle. In the middle of a green lawn stood a dwarf Japanese maple, its leaves turned red and its delicate musician's fingers trembling in the gentle breeze. A flowerbed by the main entrance burst with pale-violet aster and heavy light-blue blossoms of hydrangea reaching down almost to the ground. On the building's facade was a little sign that read, *Rest Home for People with Impaired Vision*. It was an establishment for the blind, most likely, but the prohibitions of militant public optimism had evidently banished the word *blind* from use there. Yet whatever the estate's true purpose, it was now empty.

Behind its main building began a stand of ponderosa pines. A soft light radiated from their long needles gathered in tight, elegant, low-growing clusters, and their yellowish-brown bark gave off a vanilla-like scent. High over my head an eagle soared beneath the clouds. Its thin, plaintive screech seemed to hang in the sky all by itself, independently of the powerful bird. I recalled seeing two eagles the previous spring clutching each other in the air with their talons. Unable to release their fatal grip and spread their wings in time, they fell into the ocean like a stone.

A trail rose steeply through the pines and I followed it. Somewhere in the distance I heard what sounded like a waterfall. Ten minutes later the trail made a sharp turn and brought me to a broad mountain stream.

Its icy, crystal-clear water rushed down, in places exposing its pebbly, multicoloured bottom. Moving through the water were crimson flashes. I went closer. The stream was seething with fish of a bright purple-red colour. It seemed that the elements of fire and water had been combined in one. Swimming torches, igniting the rushing water, were moving in stubborn schools against the current.

I had heard a lot about that astounding phenomenon of nature, and now I was an accidental witness of Pacific salmon returning to spawn in the same mountain stream where they were born. Outpacing each other, the big fiery fish can leap out of the water by as much as two meters to soar over rapids, logs, and other obstacles on their way to . . . to their death. By a cruel dictate of nature, the instinct in salmon species for procreation and death has become a single thing. Only once in their lives may wild salmon spawn, after which they die.

Every stage of that cycle is a mystery.

Salmon are born in shallow mountain streams from which they begin their long path to the ocean, swimming many hundreds of kilometers down with the current. And then their first metamorphosis takes place: the adaptation of their organisms to salt water. But how does that happen? Scientists have determined that the hormonal changes needed for the passage from fresh to salt water are stimulated by the lengthening of the day, and indeed the migration of salmon smolt from rivers to the sea does occur in the spring.

During the several years of their life in the ocean, salmon eat their fill, gain weight, and grow up to a meter in length. During that time their silvery light-blue scales are not much different in colour from those of other fish. But then the time comes for them to set out on the return path to their source. Again their hormones are activated, this time ensuring a reverse adaptation from salt to fresh water. And then a most striking change also takes place. Over the long weeks of contending with the current, rapids, and waterfalls, the salmon's scales will turn from a silvery blue to bright red, the same colour as their roe. In sockeye salmon, the fish's head even turns green, the upper jaw of the males grows longer and produces a downward hook called a kype, and teeth emerge, giving the fish a hideous grinning expression. But why are the teeth for? After all, it is known that during the long, arduous weeks of return to their birth places and spawning and death the salmon eat nothing. All their strength is spent on the struggle for the life of the next generation.

And how among hundreds of mountain rivers and streams do salmon find the ones where they were born? And why do they try to go only there and not to another mountain river or stream? Is it like someone who has lived a long time in a foreign land who wants to return to his native place to die? Metaphysics has no place in the arsenal of scientific investigation, and so far there has been no answer to that question. But the secret of how they find heir native rivers has, it seems, been discovered. Ichthyologists believe the fish use the earth's magnetic pole to orient themselves in the ocean, and they find the river in which they were born by its taste and chemical composition, information that had been stored in their memories in infancy.

At last the goal is attained. After traveling hundreds of kilometers against the current and over obstacles and climbed by as much as two kilometers above sea level, female salmon hollow out a depression in shallow water with their fins and deposit their eggs. The males fertilize the eggs and the females then cover them up with sand. By that time all the life forces of the salmon of both sexes have been exhausted. Making no provision for their restoration, nature immediately releases the mechanism of death: a programmed collapse of the fishes' internal organs.

Eagles then swoop down on the free banquet. Snatching the injured, tattered red carcasses from the water presents no difficulty, even if a large, healthy fish in the previously migrating mass might have been able to resist. And indeed I saw such a fish drag an eagle after itself back into the rushing water..

I didn't know eagles could swim. Gripping the fish with its powerful talons, the eagle swam "butterfly-style," first lifting its wings out of the water, then immersing them again. It was the first time I had seen a bald eagle up close. Its beak was bright yellow, the plumage of its body was a dark chocolate-brown, and its head, neck, and tail were white, the white head giving it its figurative name.

Jumping from rock to rock, I ran down along the stream, hoping to see the battle's end, but the current was so strong that the raider and its victim were soon carried out of sight.

2

A hundred meters or so downhill around a bend, the stream was wider and calmer, becoming a small river. Looking like crimson ribbons with green tips, the fish there were moving more calmly in the same dense schools, shoulder to shoulder so to speak, and ascending cement steps that had been secured to the river bottom. Such ladders are installed to help the salmon bypass dams and other steep obstacles. People assist them in a more decisive way, too. In some places the fish are scooped out of the water and taken upstream by truck to their spawning grounds.

Further downstream just below the ladder, I saw an old man of about eighty. He was standing by the water's edge making odd movements. He bowed repeatedly, raised his hands to the sky, and then sat down in a strangely awkward way. He was so absorbed in those activities that he didn't notice me, or at least pretended that he hadn't. I stopped and began to watch.

He was barefoot and terribly thin. His legs with their aged veins extended from under his faded cut-off jeans like crooked poles. All his hair had migrated from his bare head to his face, covering it with grey tufts from his chin to his eyes. Next to him on the shingle lay a faded baseball cap with the words, *Save the World*. A shabby leather jerkin hung loosely over a gaudy turtle-neck sweater that not only had been out of fashion for some fifty years but was completely out of keeping with its owner's wild appearance. Then I looked closer. What I had taken for a turtleneck were tattoos. Their multicoloured designs covered his aged body from his neck to his wrists.

Over his tattooed chest hung chains with amulets of some kind. The largest one, shaped like a wheel with woven string inside and feathers outside, I took to be a dreamcatcher like those found among native peoples from Canada to Mexico. Concluding his strange ritual or dance, the old man stepped to the side, turning with an obvious discomfort, picked up his baseball cap, pulled it down over his head, and lowered himself onto the shingle. Resting his rough, gnarled hands on his knees, he turned his face again towards the river.

"Hello, there!" I called out. I'm lost. . . I made a wrong turn, which got me to the river! So many fish! I've never seen anything like it!"

"What's that?" the old man replied, turning back towards me and cupping his palm by his ear. "Speak louder! I can't hear you over the water!"

"A lot of fish, I said!"

"A salmon run is why," he growled and turned back to look at the water. He clearly had no wish to talk to me. But I wasn't going to leave. The old man interested me.

"An amazing spectacle! But tell me, you were doing exercises.. . What were they? Tai chi or maybe kung fu?" I shouted, trying to be heard over the rushing stream.

The old man measured me with a glance but didn't reply. Then, moving sideways like a crab, he got up, extended his arms to the river in a gesture of respect, bowed several times, and then lowered himself back down on the shingle.

"It wasn't your tai chi, but a sacred salmon dance," he said at last.

"I didn't understand. What kind of dance?"

"I'm sure you buy salmon. Who's going to thank it?"

"Thank whom? The fish?"

"What did you think? It swims to us every year and offers itself for nourishment. I can grab one here with my bare

17

hands and it won't resist."

I could hardly keep from giggling.

"You think it comes here for us on purpose?"

"If not for us, who? Certainly not for itself! The fish understand everything. We bipedal nitwits don't want to know about anything but our gadgets and are proud of it, but the salmon is a wise creature."

The old man looked at me with a sly squint that completely mystified me. Was he possibly laughing at me, or was he serious? Or maybe he was just pretending to be simple-minded. . . Out there, far from the city, there are lots of eccentrics.

"After you eat it, the salmon, you should return its bones to the river. That's how it is!"

The old man pressed his clenched fists against his chest, and then, opening them, thrust them away from himself as if he were tossing something into the water. "If you leave out even one bone, the salmon will take offense and not come back. Our First-Nation brothers knew that and followed the law."

"Even though he's draped with amulets, there's something about him that isn't like a native person," it involuntarily occurred to me. Local natives have fleshy, olive faces with broad cheekbones and dark, wide-set eyes. The old man had light-coloured eyes, a narrow face, rather small features, and a duck-like nose. Native people, as a rule, are beardless and rarely bald, but here everything was the other way around.

"Well, since you've come to us, why don't you take a

seat" the old man said, suddenly relenting and indicating a place on the shingle, as if the riverbank and the river and its fish were his home. "My name's Stan. Since you're interested, I'll share a legend with you. What's your name?"

"Marina."

The old man grinned.

"You don't say! What are you, a mooring or a harbour, then? I have a boat not far from here in a 'marina'. When spring comes I'll go north or to the Fraser River for three months of fishing."

"Aren't there any fish here?"

"Well, these fish belong to the Salish. If you take them, it's like stealing. And there are too many people on the Sunshine Coast anyway. Developers and others have come. But there in the north, it's completely different. But where are you from? Your accent says that you aren't from here."

"I'm from Russia."

"You're kidding! From what city?"

"Moscow."

"Speak louder, I can't hear.

"From Moscow!"

"Really? From Moscow itself? Well, how is it there in Moscow? Moscow's at war. What are people saying? Are they against it?"

"They aren't saying anything."

"Hmm. In the States we protested during the Viet

Nam war, we planted bombs, but in your country they're what—scared?"

"Of course, they're scared. In Russia you can go to prison for opposition. But I left that place a long time ago. I live in Vancouver now."

"Aah. I know only one word in Russian: NYET! NYET!" the old man said with a chuckle.

"I need to find the ferry, but there aren't any signs—to keep me from getting lost again."

"The ferry's only twenty minutes from here. You turned left when you should have gone straight for another three kilometers and then turned."

"Maybe I can still make it."

The old man looked up at the sun weakly shining through the clouds and shook his head.

"You won't. The ferry will cast off in fifteen minutes. The next one will be in two hours."

Since I had time to kill, I sat down on the shingle near him. He pulled from a pocket of his cut-offs a little metal box, took from it a pinch of grass, got out of another pocket some rolling papers, rolled a joint, lit it, and took a drag. The sickeningly sweet smell of marijuana floated in my direction.

"Here," Stan said, extending the joint to me after he had taken another drag.

"Thank you, I don't smoke."

"It's up to you, of course, but a mistake. The juices flow more merrily through your veins from this grass. You want to

sing! You want to dance! You say that the salmon dance is a
strange one. But I'll tell you, I lived for a while with the Salish
at the very tip of Vancouver Island. That's their land, their
domain. I worked together with them in a cannery. I rented
a room from a pal and his old woman. She still remembered
their language and could speak it and knew spells but talked in
English with us, of course. We would come back from work,
his lady would put on a pot of fish soup and tell us stories.
How the Salish believe that there is a salmon nation in the
world. A mighty nation, with chiefs and elders, who all live
in longhouses on a distant island. One time the salmon nation
heard that the Salish were dying of hunger. The nation decided
to turn into fish and place itself at the mercy of people. And so
it went until after a time the salmon nation changed its mind
about going up mountain rivers and streams, and people had
nothing to eat. What could they do? The Salish decided to
find the salmon nation and say to it, "Save our children from
hunger, return in the autumn to our rivers." Well, they fitted
out a kayak, gathered as many gifts as they could put into it,
including various kinds of medicinal herbs, but they still didn't
know where to go. Then the sun told them: there, at the end
of the ocean is an island, where the salmon nation lives in
longhouses. Good. The Salish sailed to the island. They saw
a village, houses, and totem poles. The salmon tribe received
their guests well, and as was their custom arranged a feast for
them. And during the feast, the chief of the salmon tribe, their
king, ordered four of his brothers to go into the ocean. As the

brothers were entering the water, they immediately turned into fish. The chief caught the fish and fed them to his guests. The guests ate their fill and, as was their way, threw the fish bones back into the ocean. And immediately the brothers turned into people again. Well, they did and they didn't, since they emerged from the water as cripples: one had part of his face missing, another, his arms. Somebody among the guests hadn't thrown all his bones back into the ocean, you see, but had hidden them. But when he returned those bones to the ocean, the salmon-men were completely whole again. So it happened! While you ... "

I remained silent. Stan looked at me expectantly. Something in the irregular features of his face unsettled me. His eyes were too close together, giving him an expression of owl-like perplexity.

Then I couldn't help myself.

"A beautiful legend. But sheer paganism!"

Stan grinned.

"Paganism? But weren't the ancient Greeks pagans too? All those satyrs and dryads ... How was that any different?"

"I'm sorry, but you ... How to put it ... "

"Go ahead, don't be afraid ... "

"Do you actually believe that legend?"

"I don't believe in legends, or in any religion, or in paganism, or in any of that suff. Religion, like any ideology, has one purpose—to take away people's freedom. To deprive them of choice. But I'm free."

And he again took a drag and sent a sickeningly sweet stream of smoke in my direction.

He had completely confused me.

"Then why were you ... making those movements before? Why were you dancing?"

"Maybe I was a salmon king in a former life, who knows? And the time will then come for me to go back to my people, when they won't turn me away from the gate but allow me to enter my home.

And he grinned again and again blew more smoke from his stinking hand-rolled cigarette.

That completely befuddled me. Was the old man joking or serious? It was clear in any case hat he enjoying my confusion.

"Niels Bohr had a horseshoe nailed to his door. He was asked, 'Can you, a physicist, really believe in horseshoes?' And he answered, 'No, I don't. But whether I believe in it or not, it could still bring me luck.'"

I didn't understand anything! How could Stan know about Niels Bohr?

"What, did I confuse you? I'm not what you thought I was? Yes, I'm a physicist by education. I was born in Seattle. Only I gave up physics. It wasn't for me. And that was during the Viet Nam era and obligatory military service. Who wants to die for no known reason? I slipped away to Canada with a pal. The Canadians accepted draft dodgers with open arms. They were all against the war, too. A Canadian border officer even called a taxi for me and gave me some money so I could get to the nearest town."

"Have you never had an urge to go back?"

"Well, what can I tell you? When Carter announced a pardon for draft evaders, yes, I could have gone back. And I thought about it."

"But you stayed? You must have fallen in love with a Canadian girl, right?"

The old man grinned again.

"Exactly. I did fall in love. With the Canadian north. It grabbed me with its cold claws and wouldn't let me go. And turned me into an ... aborigine! Ha-ha! And now I wander. Three months in a boat, and in the fall and winter here in a bus."

"You travel around by bus?" I asked, not understanding.

"What for? My own bus has served me for ages. A school bus. You know, a yellow one. They retired it and I bought it cheap. I reequipped it with a stove and a refrigerator and live in it commune-style with no rent—for nothing. Ha-ha!"

"But how much do you have to pay to park it?"

Stan shook his head:

"Nada! A pal of mine here owns a five-hectare forest. He and I have an understanding. I'm young, ha-ha, but he's already an old man and feeble, even though he's ten years younger than I am! I chop firewood for him, fix whatever needs fixing, and for that he gives me the land ... under my bus. 'Stan, park your jalopy on my parcel, only far away from my house so that egg yolk will be out of my sight. Or repaint it green,' he says. Well, I parked it down below his house behind a cliff next to a brook, thank goodness!"

The old man sighed and shook his head.

"And so I'll live there until spring and then I'll go to the Fraser River. I have a brother there in the river. I haven't seen him for a long time. Around three years. If he's still alive."

"Your brother?"

"Yes! He's a sturgeon, the king of fish. The oldest fresh-water fish in the world. It's said that they used to catch sturgeon six meters long weighing half a ton, but now they've mostly disappeared because of the dam. I caught my brother three years ago and released him. He was close to two hundred kilos, for certain."

"But how did you catch him?"

"How I did will be my secret. I didn't pull him up to the surface, you see, but only looked at him. Since fish, especially ocean fish, can't be returned if they come from a great depth. The difference in pressure will kill them."

"How did the sturgeon get to be so big?"

"By not scurrying about. They lie on the bottom gathering wisdom and can live for a hundred years. But now they're toxic. We've dumped poisons in the rivers, and they collect them from the bottom. So that I'll get to see him . . only if my brother's alive. But I only fish for salmon and then only as much as I can eat, and leave the rest for the bears."

"Do you mean that there could be bears here too?"

"They haven't disappeared yet. Whenever a salmon run begins, the bears come down from the mountains to catch the fish. When it starts to get dark, expect visitors."

I involuntarily glanced around. The sun was still quite high. On both sides of the river there were stands of spruce. They were especially dense along the riverbank. I had read somewhere that fish skeletons left by feasting bears serve as excellent fertilizer for spruce growing along the riverbanks. The trees secure the soil with their roots and help maintain the cool river temperatures that salmon need for spawning. I wanted to display my erudition, but felt shy about it.

The old man finished smoking, stood up, stretched, and then limped over to the water and started groping in it. He moved his hands here and there and then pulled out a large fish.

"See, it's quite shallow here. Big ones like this get stuck and can't go any further. But I'll just tickle its belly and it will immediately jump up and leap onto the ladder by itself. Here, you try it!"

He held out a huge, trembling salmon with its awful grimace.

"Oh no, thank you!"

"Scared? But it won't bite. You just tickle its belly like this and immediately all the anguish will pass. You'll feel at peace. People in the cities are searching for the meaning of life, while here it is, that meaning!"

He threw the fish back into the water closer to the

ladder, and it merged with the school.

"Of course, the salmon here are having a difficult time, it's true, but the fish are still free. Despite the ladder, they really don't depend on anybody. And I love that. Not like the ones from the hatcheries—a hopeless case!"

"How is it different?" I asked in surprise.

"The hatchery fry can't find their way to the ocean by themselves, that's how. A lost generation!" the old man grinned.

The sky was starting to frown. A light rain had begun to fall, and it immediately got colder.

I looked at my watch.

"Go how I told you. About three kilometers, and then a turn. Make sure you don't miss it."

I was sorry to leave that mountain stream and its salmon nation. And I didn't want to part with that strange, mysterious old man either.

Looking for a pretext to linger, I said,

"It was good to meet you. I learned a lot of interesting things from you. Thank you! Only in saying good-bye, I wanted to ask: that talisman around your neck ... Is it a dreamcatcher? I've seen them in souvenir shops, but yours is more interesting."

"What have shops got to do with it!" the old man said in obvious dismay. "A shaman gave it to me. It's a soul-catcher. When I was young, I was working as a lumberjack near Whitehorse. I fell from a big Douglas fir. I couldn't stand for a month. Both my femurs were dislocated. I was close to the other world, but a local shaman returned my soul to me with this wheel. My soul's time had not yet come. He said, 'Don't part with this talisman, but when your time does come, return it to the salmon king. He himself will swim to you, only you'll have to recognize him among the other fish—don't miss him. He will accept you back into your home.'"

The old man sighed and fell silent.

"Go, go," he said after a pause without looking in my direction, "or else you'll miss the next ferry."

After I left I turned around to look back at him. Stan was still gazing at the mountain stream. It was as if I no longer existed or was no longer in his orbit.

But there was the same unceasing, eternal sound of the mountain stream and the bright crimson flashes of fish straining towards birth and death.

Rapture

1

"You know that I love you."

"Yes. You've told me. Many times."

"Remember, you're not alone in this city. I'm just a phone call away."

Ralph raised his fingers, thrust his hands forward, his gold cufflinks catching the candlelight, pushed his plate a few inches away, and then rearranged the already perfectly arranged cutlery. Like many short men in positions of authority, he felt a need to enhance his physical presence by taking control of space and making more room for himself.

"As I said, no matter where I am, you can always call me. I'm off to London next week. But if something happens, you can always depend on me."

"But . . .what could happen?

"I'm not saying anything will. But if you need anything, I'll always be at my hotel in the evening, working. The time difference between London and Vancouver is ... let's see ... eight hours—not so bad. If you call me in the morning, your morning, that will be the best time for me."

"But I ... I really don't need anything."

"Yes, you do! Of course you do! If you'd like me to, I can talk to one our partners here. They may need a secretary."

"That's very kind of you, Ralph, but I'm ... I'm no good

at that sort of thing."

"What do you mean, no good? You can do anything you want. Anything you apply yourself to. See what I'm saying?"

"I don't understand technical stuff, Ralph, and besides ... secretarial work really isn't for me."

"You don't need to be good with tech for that kind of work. You know how to type. You can schedule meetings, right? You're good with people ... when you want to be. Even with me, sometimes ... tee-hee. When you're in the right mood, I mean, tee-hee."

His interlaced fingers resting on his belly, he rapidly twiddled his thumbs, a habit that he usually combined with a chuckle and a cough."

You need some steady income, tee-hee, that's the thing."

"You're telling me!"

"Don't be angry, Maya. I'm just trying to help ... Once you have some income, you can start looking for a better job, that's all I'm saying. One thing can lead to another. When you lost your CBC job, did you ask them if there was anything in a different department or even part-time?"

"There was no point. I didn't have enough seniority, which is why they laid me off. Along with hundreds of other people."

"Did you even try?"

"Try what? To humiliate myself? I know someone from the newsroom who was rehired as a freelancer. The same amount of work for a fraction of his previous salary. That's not for me, thank you."

"But he might get something better there in the future. See, that was your strategic mistake. You had two young kids and should have asked. Never give up, never! Well, there's no point in going back over it now. You were a radio journalist, a producer. Couldn't you have switched to a newspaper or something? Also, no? Okay. But what happened with your teaching? You had steady work at two colleges. Why did you give that up? You never told me."

"It doesn't matter."

"Well, go back to them. Ask them if they have an opening."

"They've probably already hired somebody else."

"See? You're assuming things. But life can surprise you. As I said, never surrender. Good wine, eh? Want to know how I earned my first buck? Buying for two dollars and selling for four, not bad for a twelve- year-old, eh? I was quite the little dealer. Hee-hee."

"I'm sure you were."

"Look, I'm not suggesting that you have to sell lemonade. But you could sell bolsters, for example."

"Sell what?"

"Yoga pads, bolsters, whatever you use for your classes. What do they pay you per hour?"

"It depends on the studio. Twenty dollars, usually."

"That's what I'm talking about. You can't make a living

that way. *You* have to hire people, not ask people to hire you. Start your own business, and once you have your own studio, you can organize a little shop on the side. That's additional income. Somebody comes for a class but forgot to bring a mat. No problem! You have them for sale!"

"But business isn't for me, Ralph. I don't want to manage a studio. If I can't do what I really want, at least I can teach yoga for the time being."

"Hold on! How do you know you're not good at it if you don't even try? You know what your problem is?"

"I'm sure I have more than one."

"Your low self-esteem. That's the first thing we have to fix. Every morning when you get up, stand in front of the mirror and say, 'I am capable of anything. I am beautiful and I am smart. I am beautiful and I am smart.' You say it ten times."

"And then what? I become beautiful?"

"You already are. What you lack is self-confidence. Let's look into it. If I can help you rent some space not exactly downtown, but close enough, say for ten to fifteen students, how much would the rent be? How many employees would you need, and how much could you afford to pay them? You need a business plan."

"I'm going to scream."

"Please, don't be mad at me, Maya. It was only a suggestion."

"I'm not mad at you. I'm simply trying to tell you that ... that ... And you don't ... I'm trying to tell you that I'm good at teaching yoga, and that's what I'm going to do now, as long as I have energy for four classes a day. So let's drop it, please."

The restaurant on the top floor of the forty-two-story Empire Landmark Hotel, one the tallest buildings in Vancouver until its demolition in 2019, was slowly revolving. The lights on the mountains of the North Shore, separated from Vancouver by the dark streak of Burrard Inlet, slowly shifted in the twilight. The Downtown peninsula, with the dark cedars and firs of Stanley Park at its tip, likewise receded from view, while the downtown core, a blaze of twinkling lights, appeared to move toward us.

"You're not going back to Montréal, are you?" Ralph asked, as he poured me another glass of Cabernet.

"Obviously not. Why?"

"A department of our agency has been looking for a Russian instructor. We're collaborating on some projects with Russian astronauts. You could teach Russian, couldn't you?"

"Good lord!" I said, putting down my glass. "Why are you asking me that now?"

"Oh, it just came up. Their instructor is going on maternity leave, I was told." He paused. "Well, it would only be a temporary position anyway, not what you need. You don't like the wine? You liked it last time, I remember."

"I don't feel like drinking right now. I need to get home soon."

"I'll give you a ride, don't worry. Tomorrow is Sunday. You don't have classes, do you?"

"No, not on Sunday."

"I'd like to see you tomorrow," he said quietly, then paused for a moment and gave me a bold, penetrating look that brooked no objections. "We can go for a walk in Stanley Park. I've only been there once. I'll be busy in the morning, but I can free up my afternoon ... for you."

I didn't reply. Ralph poured himself another glass of wine and sat back, his fingers lightly drumming on the table.

"Tell me something. Did you leave Montréal because of me?"

"No. But you were a big part of my decision, if you really have to know."

His outstretched fingers froze in the air.

"Ah! You wanted to get away from me so badly that you fled to the other side of the continent with no job, no connections—just left, as far away from terrible Ralph as possible?"

"Well, at least I tried. Obviously, not very successfully."

"You don't pull any punches, do you."

"What can I say? You asked me a direct question and I gave you a direct answer."

An ugly little creature stirred within me, filling me with anger. The little monster wanted to punish Ralph for his dogged kindness; for the cushy job at the Space Agency that might have given me—if only temporarily—some relief but had gone to somebody else (never mind that I had already left the city); for his sloping shoulders that moved up and down when he chuckled; for his small, pale, well-manicured hands; for his tidy little feet in their expensive leather shoes.

I gazed out the window. The city was flaunting itself with arrogant indifference, as if I were an incidental visitor in no way related to its picture-perfect mountains, beaches, and bays, all of them disappearing in the encroaching darkness that was softening the harshness of day-time glass and steel. The high-rises, silhouetted against the indigo sky, were ablaze with lights. Down below in the deep canyons between them, fireflies of cars flitted about.

"Am I really so repulsive to you, Maya?" Ralph said as he fingered his striped yellow and black tie. His blue eyes gazed at me with childish helplessness.

"You're a good person, Ralph, and I know you really care for me and I appreciate it ... But I just can't ... I just don't share your feelings."

"And if I had been free, would that have changed things in any way?"

"You know the answer ... We've been over it many times. Why torture us both? I can be a friend to you, and I am. I respect your knowledge, your abilities, but for the rest, I just don't have it in me, whatever it takes."

"Whatever it takes? I'm not asking you for anything. I'm not asking you for sex."

"Oh, you're asking for a lot more than that! But I can only give you what I have. And what I don't have, I can't give you. And there's nothing, nothing in the world I can do about that! Don't you understand?"

"Yes, you've made it quite clear."

"Then why do you keep ... ?"

"It's called cognitive dissonance."

Although usually quick in speech and movement and bristling with busy energy, Ralph suddenly froze, as if a mechanism inside him had suddenly broken. For a moment, he stared at the plate of hors d'oeuvres. Then he quickly wiped his mouth with his starched napkin, put the napkin down on the table, pushed his chair back, and abruptly got up.

"I'll be right back," he said brusquely.

"I'm sorry! I didn't mean ... "

"There's nothing to be sorry about. It isn't your fault," he said without looking at me.

Relieved to be alone, I took a book from my purse. It was a multilingual anthology of poets from different countries who wrote around the turn of the last century, including Valery Bryusov, a founder of Russian Symbolism. The author of the book's preface was quoting a memoir of Bryusov by one of the young poets in his circle: "The *maître* demanded an ardent way of living from us ... Every day, every waking hour, in fact, we had to search for transcendence, for rapture. We had to seek a light that would transform our souls, that would lead to a revelation. Hunters of illusive images, intoxicated without intoxicants, we turned ourselves into somnambulists who ... "

"What are you reading, if I may ask?" I heard Ralph's

voice as he leaned over my shoulder.

I quickly shut the book.

"Nothing in particular."

"Oh, please, Maya. Why are you so secretive about your reading. I'm not a complete idiot, you know. I read books too. "

"Of course you do. I just don't think this one is your cup of tea."

"Try me."

"If you insist. This we'll skip ... And this one too ... Well, maybe this. It's by Rubén Darío, a Nicaraguan poet. A prose fragment from his "El Velo de la Reina Mab" or "The Veil of Queen Mab.""

"Why are you interested in him?"

Again, I felt a tightness in my chest, an urge to rebel.

"Why? For no good reason, as you will probably think. I'm going to write a book about him, that's the reason. I'm going to write a book about a poet you know nothing about. Well, a poet many people here know nothing about. An influential figure, the founder of *modernismo.* That's why. You don't think I could do it?"

Ralph looked at his watch.

"I never said you couldn't. But you have to prioritize things. Steady income first, and then hobbies and artsy things ... What's going on here? What happened to the next course? We've been waiting fifteen minutes already."

He snapped his fingers, trying to get the server's

attention, then impatiently started to move things around on the table.

"Why don't you read to me while we wait."

"It's in Spanish, of course. But here's a rough prose translation.

"'Queen Mab rose in her chariot cut from a single pearl and waved her veil, barely tangible, as if it had been woven from the breath of dreams—sweet dreams—and through her veil life was immersed in a rosy light... . She covered with her veil all four of them: emaciated, desperate, yet bold. And their sorrows left them and hope settled in their hearts, and in their heads, a merry sun and the cunning imp of pride that dwells in poor artists even in their moments of despair. And since then, azure dreams have reigned in the garrets of those poor misfits, and the days have seemed radiant, laughter has chased away their sorrows, and a wild *farandole* has whirled before white Apollo in the form of a glistening canvas, a dilapidated violin, and a faded manuscript.'"

"Hmm. What's that all about? Artists building castles in the air? That's what makes them happy? I'm just a simple person. I could never understand such things. Will you teach me?" Ralph said with an ingratiating smile.

"Teach you? You know so much more than I do! What could I teach you?"

"What you just read. You know why I love you? Why I can never be angry with you? Because you live in the world that I don't understand. But when I'm with you, it feels like

I'm going to a different place ... And in a moment something new will open up in me," he said with a sigh. "Or maybe I'm just fooling myself. Like your poor artists. Feeding on an illusion. When did he live, your Rubén Darío?

"He died in 1916."

"That's a long time ago."

"Do you know what my own name means in Sanskrit? An illusion or dream ... "

"Well ... you're not my illusion. You're my obsession."

The next course finally arrived. Ralph flipped his tie to the side and pounced on his steak—he was obviously hungry. I looked at his strong healthy teeth, his neatly trimmed, greying goatee, his bald patch with silver in its rim of once dark and curly hair. His was not an unattractive face. From time to time, he would lift his bright blue eyes to me. They expressed his irrepressible vitality and enjoyment of food, wine, and the world around him. But I knew how quick-tempered he could be, how peremptory when what he thought was his due was not immediately granted, and how impatient he was with those who failed to understand things that his quick mind had already grasped. He was a talented physicist who was responsible for an enormous budget and hundreds of people. He did not spare himself and was used to long hours of work, and he expected the same from others. He had successfully channeled his prodigious energy towards the achievement of his goals, managing complex projects and bending the will of others will to his needs.

"Do you hear anything from Alex in Moscow?" Ralph asked.

"No.

"Hmm ... And your older son?"

"Michael? He rarely calls. Busy with his student's life, I suppose."

"Doesn't call his mom?"

"He doesn't like Waterloo ... "

"So what? It isn't that hard to make a phone call ... Waterloo has the best undergraduate math program in Canada. He should appreciate what you've done for him. By the way, Aaron calls every week from Harvard. If he didn't, he would get hell from his mom and he knows it. Ha-ha!"

"I taught my children to be independent. Maybe too independent ... How is Malka doing, by the way?" I was feeling more and more lonely as the evening progressed.

"Malka? Oh, fine, fine!" Ralph cut up his steak into neat little squares and sent one after another into his mouth, washing them down with a sips of wine.

"Hmm, nice steak, very nice. Cooked just right! Want to try some? No? How's your fish? Did I tell you Malka graduated with straight A's? I'm sending her to Europe for two months. My graduation present."

"By herself?"

"Oh, no! Her mother would never allow that. All three are going, Esther and both kids. And then I'll join them for a couple of weeks after a conference in London."

I wondered how my phone calls would fit into that plan.

"We're going to spend a week in Greece, then in Italy, and then in Israel. I'll have to return home to work, but Esther will stay on in Israel for another month with the kids, visiting relatives."

Why was he telling me all that? Was I his sister? One of his wife's friends? Ah, letting me know that he was going to be free for a whole month, that's why.

"I thought it was time to arrange a holiday for the whole family. Esther complains that I practically live in Montréal now. But what can I do? I can't move the Space Agency to Toronto, can I?"

"Do you still go back to Toronto every weekend?"

"It works out to a little more than a weekend, since I leave Montréal on Thursday. That's Thursday, Friday, Saturday and Sunday—almost four days that I'm with my family. But it doesn't seem to be enough lately. I can see my wife's point. I've been commuting back and forth for how long? Almost eight years ... "

"That's hard," I said in a neutral tone.

"Well, I've optimized the process. I don't pack. Everything I need is duplicated in both places. I travel only with a briefcase."

"Couldn't you move your family to Montréal?

"A difficult proposition. Esther has all her friends in Toronto. Then there's the synagogue, of which we've both have been members for decades. Esther runs an educational program there. She's on several boards. The kids had their bar and bat mitzvahs there. I said Kaddish for my father there after he died, and he had his *yahrzeit* just before I came to Vancouver."

"What exactly is Kaddish?"

"A prayer for the departed. I went to the synagogue to pray every morning for a year, as is the custom. When I was in Montréal, I went to Beth Zion. I just finished recently. And felt better for it."

"For a whole year? How did you manage that with your schedule?"

"You do what you have to do... I loved my father, you see. I was very close to him. I miss him terribly. But when you pray, you're not alone. You're part of a *minyan*, a community. It becomes your support group. And it helped me to cope ... to cope with my grief, you see." Ralph looked away, his eyes misting over.

"I didn't know you were so religious. Being a scientist, I mean."

"Theoretically, you can't prove the existence of God. But you can't disprove it either," he said.

Ralph finished chewing and then moved his tongue around inside his mouth, evidently checking for bits of meat that might be stuck between his teeth.

"Would you like some dessert? Some coffee? No? I'll tell you what, then. Why don't we go down to my room? I have a present for you."

"You really shouldn't be buying me presents."

"Why shouldn't I? It's your birthday."

"It's next week, not today."

"But I won't be here next week. Come on. It's still early."

2

A suite with heavy executive-style furniture that smelled of disinfectants. Ralph took off his navy-blue blazer with shiny metal buttons and hung it on the back of an armchair. I noted his suspenders and looked away.

A standing lamp responded to the pressure of his foot, illuminating a nondescript abstract picture on the wall and casting concentric circles on the grey carpet. A cardboard box on the coffee table contained my birthday present, a clunky vase of ornamental crystal.

"Nice, don't you think? I love glass! May I kiss the birthday girl?"

I held out my cheek to him.

"'That's all I get? Put the vase down. Let's sit for a moment." He indicated the sofa and after sitting down beside me took my hand in his.

I reached for lipstick in my purse, the only pretext I could think of to free my hand.

"You don't need lipstick, darling. If I wanted to kiss

you, you think the lipstick would stop me? Please put it away."

I hesitated, then returned it to my purse.

"Now tell me what's going on, Maya. Why are you in such an awful mood today? Did I do or say something wrong? We had a nice meal. Your birthday is coming. What can I do to make you happy? Shall I put on some music? Let's see, there must be a radio somewhere."

"No music, please!"

"You don't like music?"

"I hate music, any kind of music, as you might remember. And I'm not in a bad mood. Actually, I'm in an excellent mood! It's funny when I think about it. Truly funny!" I said, unable to keep from laughing.

"What is so funny?"

"It's hilarious! I just imagined you sweating over your drawing board with your sleeves rolled up."

"Nobody uses drawing boards anymore, Maya."

"Whatever. No, it's really funny. Such a difficult project! A hard nut to crack! Ralph is sweating away! But he's a problem solver. Will he ever give up? No, never! The rocket must be launched! He's thrashing around, trying out this and that—no luck! Grr–Grr-puff-puff! Fumes everywhere, tram-tara-tram! Boom-boom! One technical problem after another. It's completely stuck! But Ralph is stubborn. He'll get if off the ground, even if it kills him."

"What on earth are you talking about?"

"You and me."

"You think that's funny?"

"Isn't it?"

Ralph shook his head from side to side while loosening his tie as if it was strangling him. He walked over to the window and folded his arms across his chest.

I went up to him and touched his shoulder. "I'm sorry if I hurt your feelings, Ralph. I didn't mean to ... Really."

"Well of course you did. Of course you did," he said without turning around. "But I deserved it."

"No, it's just ... You're right ... I'm not in the best of moods. We've known each other for how long? Three years or more? And you still haven't given up. The stamina ... All the energy you spend on me ... But why? Why? I'm an ordinary woman. I don't know what you see in me! Why did you even start talking to me that time on the train? A good-looking woman by herself, so you decided to try your luck?"

"Enough, Maya. Enough! I'm not a womanizer! I don't pick up good-looking women on trains, as you're perfectly well aware. But if you really want to know what happened to me on that train when I saw you for the first time, I'll tell you. You were sitting alone, next to a window. I don't know how to put it, but there was such an aura of resignation about you ... As if you had completely given up. I asked you something and you replied. Automatically, without paying any attention to me. But then you raised your eyes. I'll never forget that moment. There was a silent plea for help in them. I fell in love with you then and there. I know you well enough by now. Even if you need me, you'll never show it and always keep your equanimity, too proud to admit any weakness. You can be stubborn, you can get angry with me and say nasty things, then regret it and take your words back. It can be confusing sometimes. I don't know what you really want. No, not true. I do know. But look, no matter what you say, I still see the vulnerable girl in you just as I did that first time. And I want to protect you. To love you the best I can. It's a hopeless task. I know that too. And I'm lost, lost in a way that I've never been in my life. Understand?"

3

Where exactly did those crumbling steps in Trastevere lead? Maya couldn't remember now. Up and up, past a tangle of climbing roses, ivy, and wisteria covering ancient walls on both sides. Five steps ahead of her, without looking back, Al was ascending in quick strides, easily carrying his lithe, long-limbed frame. Al. She liked his name:. It was a pictograph, a code to be deciphered, a magic box full of secret meanings or of different masks one could put on. Albrecht, as his Swiss father called him, or Alistair, according to his Irish mother, or Albert for stiff and indifferent people. But for her, Aleshenka, a gentle Russian verbal caress to which he responded with a pause and a chuckle. No, her Aleshenka didn't need to look back. She would follow him. Always, for the rest of her life. She didn't want to be a distraction. Let music, that great enigmatic power that consumed him, let that power rule his life, just as love for him would rule hers.

They had come to Rome at the invitation of the Orchestra Dell'Accademia Nazionale di Santa Cecilia, the most distinguished music institution in Rome. Al, a performer, composer, and conductor of international reputation, was to conduct his own symphony in the Basilica di Santa Cecilia. The work required a full orchestra and a huge choir. Sitting through the dress rehearsal, she compared it in scope to Mahler's Third, and thought how magnificent its discordant musical edifice was, if only she could understand, feel, absorb it!

But contemporary classical music didn't speak to her soul the way Bach or Haydn could. And listening to the frantic cadences that rose and fell and rose to be replaced by serene passages that were then swept away by truculent woodwinds and screeching violins, she didn't know which would be better. Should she confess to Al that this kind of music was beyond her grasp, or add her voice to the choir of his admirers, the entourage that followed him wherever he went? But that quandary didn't diminish her awe for an artist who could create, out of nothing, an edifice, a cathedral, of such complexity and scale.

In his tails, white bow tie, and white shirt in sharp contrast to his shiny charcoal-black hair, Al fitted to perfection her idea of a musical genius and conductor, the slightest twitch of whose baton was instantly obeyed by the entire orchestra. Except that he didn't use a baton. That was the conductor's choice, he explained. The orchestra could decipher with equal ease the dancing of his hands. When quite young, he said, he was lucky enough to be present at one of Stravinsky's last performances. By that time, Stravinsky was so frail that he could neither stand, nor conduct. He simply waved his baton in a haphazard way. But the musicians didn't humiliate the great man. They maintained the tempo on their own, while pretending to follow his lead.

"Show me how you do it. A couple of movements or gestures, along with what they mean."

Al smiled, then took her by the wrist and guided her hand this way and that, explaining how he communicated with the orchestra. She listened eagerly to the sound of his voice, letting the meanings of his words slip away. What remained in her memory was the sensation of his touch: his hand over her wrist, his eyes melting, the way they always did when he looked at her. Every time she remembered that, she blushed a little.

For the memorable concert at the Basilica di Santa Cecilia, she wore a flowing mauve dress with a necklace of dark amethysts that suited her complexion and light auburn hair. She knew she couldn't compete with the stylish Italian *bel mondo*—that would have taken practice and money. But Al loved her the way she was: unpolished and without money. He had given her many proofs of his affection in his quiet, undemonstrative, even gently aloof way. It was there, in the Basilica, that he introduced her as his fiancée.

She sat in the front row left of the podium during the

performance. From that vantage, Al's profile resembled Liszt's in a portrait she had seen as a child in her piano teacher's studio. Al's was a sensitive, handsome, intelligent face that reflected the ardent labor of his art. He had a high, open forehead and aquiline nose, dark, gleaming, melancholy eyes that often gazed with a slight squint over the heads of his companions, as if he could see something that was concealed from everyone else. His chivalrous old-fashioned manners enchanted women. But why, among all his female admirers, had he chosen her, a single mother of two sons, well past her prime (even if she was younger than he was by twelve years), born and raised in a different culture, a dilettante in music— why had he fallen for her?

She tried to chase away those thoughts. Her musical ignorance didn't appear to bother him. When she told him that, yes, she liked his symphony, especially the second, more lyrical part with its graceful andante that reminded her of *Giselle,* he assured her that she knew enough. Could it be, she asked, that he had been inspired by that ballet, or was the similarity only a coincidence?

He smiled, obviously enjoying the suggestion.

"You remember it well enough to remember the score too?"

Some of it, she said, especially the Dance of the Willis. That old-fashioned ballet was her favorite of the Romantic repertoire. Al's andante in the second part of his symphony was like the Dance of the Willis, the ghosts of betrayed young maidens who died on the eve of their weddings and who in revenge lure men into the forest and force them to dance to exhaustion and death.

That conversation took place in the empty Basilica after the audience and musicians had left. Al drew her closer and kissed her eyelids. "My clever girl, you do know some things, don't you?"

She was moved by his words, by that closeness under the watch of the Basilica's marble angels. Back at their hotel, she confided in a childlike whisper, slightly burring her words, that she didn't think she was clever at all. Unlike him, she still didn't know what her real vocation was. Having been a successful radio journalist and producer and now a popular university instructor didn't mean much to her because ... well, because none of it truly gripped her. What she really wanted was to devote herself to art, a goal that so far had eluded her. She wrote poetry but didn't think it was any good. She had tried her hand at prose, but doubt undermined her efforts. Did she have what it took: tenacity and the ability to say something new when everything had already been said? Disheartened, she nestled her head against his neck, hoping for encouragement.

But that's not what he gave her. Instead, she remembered clearly, when she said that she didn't think she had anything new to say, Aleshenka abruptly stepped back from her, and with a severe glance said emphatically, enunciating each word, "Don't write unless you can't help it. If it isn't a matter of life and death, *don't write*!"

She sighed audibly to let him know how real her pain was, but deep down she was grateful for his frankness. He had confirmed what she had known all along: that the torture of hunting for a will-o'-the-wisp wasn't worth it if you could live by the reflected light of someone you loved. Love was more precious, more essential, than a constant yearning for something elusive. Love was life. The rest was a chimera. By removing her burden, he was liberating her, giving her permission to live. Just live.

His words, as true as they were pitiless, pointed to a new direction, and she was ready to follow them.

4

After they had left Rome and traveled south to Bari on the Adriatic coast where Al was to give another concert, he again introduced her as his fiancée.

After the concert, an Italian conductor and colleague invited a group of about twenty people to his villa. There they ate, drank, and talked in a jolly, affable, chaotic Italian way in the courtyard under clusters of golden-yellow laburnum flowers and shrieking peacocks patrolling nearby. She marveled at the oranges you could pick from a tree in front of the villa, and at the platter of enormous green olives held by the Italian conductor—what was his first name?—as he hovered nearby with a frank and knowing gaze that made her uncomfortable, although she remembered it later with vain pleasure. In Italy, men found her attractive and didn't hide it.

The next morning, they went to look at the *trulli*, the traditional limestone houses for which Apulia is famous. The conductor insisted on accompanying them. Walking at her side, he smiled at her, complimented her fractured Italian, while Al walked ten steps ahead, as was his custom. The small, round dwellings with conical roofs sitting on top of dry stone walls made her think of Snow White's dwarfs out for a stroll. It was there by the *trulli* that a sense of unreality took hold of her with particular force. Had she been dreaming with her eyes open? Had fate inserted her as an extra in some fairy tale, while the real protagonists were busy somewhere else in the wings?

But that strange unease disappeared as soon as they were back on their own again. Proceeding north to Switzerland, their next destination, they stopped over in the small hill town of Panicale in Umbria on the eastern slope of Mount Petrarvella. The spaces inside the medieval walls surrounding the ancient fortress had been repurposed as a hotel. She tried to hide her parochial awe at the bold contrast of Italian avant-garde interior design and the ancient beams and stone.

In his white cotton pants and jacket Al looked younger than his age. He was now relaxed and his dark, wistful eyes smiled at her benevolently. They walked along the walls of the fortress to a small square with a medieval fountain. He picked up a metal rod and with boyish nonchalance tried to elicit sounds from every object on his path: the metal fence serving as a xylophone producing rough, uneven wo-wo-o-s, the trunk of an oak emitting a dull hollow moan, and a stone that refused to cooperate at all.

They left the town and walked past vineyards down towards Lake Trasimeno, a glimpse of which they had caught from their window. Al wanted to see the lake, where Hannibal's army had famously beaten the Romans during the Second Punic War.

Pines and juniper covered the slope below, and as they descended to the lake, the fresh breeze was replaced by a current of warm air caressing her face with a fragrance of pine needles. The pinks and yellows of oleander blooms and the dusty silver of olive trees enchanted her—she was in communion with that timeless world. Aleshenka was at her side, and in his presence she felt peace and contentment, as if she had been given a magic shield against the vague apprehensions and forebodings deep inside her.

Beauty in all its forms, beauty in nature and beauty in art, had always slightly dismayed her by sharpening the contrast between divine harmony and her own human imperfection. But now, because of Aleshenka, the previously impermeable boundary between herself and the world was melting away; the rough edges were being smoothed out, the questioning and discontent allayed. She had accepted the world and the world had accepted her. Al loved her and he was now her world.

As they followed he path downhill, they crossed a little brook. Al reached for a reed, stripped it clean, and blew into it, producing a coarse, dull sound. "Pan will certainly have sounded much better than that when he played his flute," he said. "He challenged Apollo himself to a musical duel. Did you knew that the flute was my first instrument and the violin my second?"

"Pan? What Pan are you talking about?"

"Wasn't there only one? Have a look! There, hiding behind the trees! See? That lovely creature with horns and hooves."

"How do you know that Pan lives here?"

"What's the name of this town, darling?"

"I see. But what exactly is he doing in our woods?"

"*His* woods, you mean. He's doing what you and I are doing. Loafing about with nary a thought in our heads. In his case, chasing nymphs and making love to them. . ." Al drew her close and kissed her cheek.

"A very chaste kiss. Can we not do Pan's?"

"It wasn't good enough? Am I to ravish you? But I can't compete with the hoofed one, my dear. I'm afraid I made my choice between Bacchus and Apollo a long time ago!"

He let her go and suddenly started galloping down the path. When she finally caught up with him, he was sitting on a boulder, gazing at the remote lake partly veiled in a milky haze. She sat down beside him and put her arm around his waist.

"What are you thinking about, Aleshenka?" she asked.

"Nothing particular. Just wondering about *L'Après-midi d'un faune*. Debussy was inspired by Mallarmé's poem of that name, of course, but maybe he visited this place too."

5

"Why don't we spend six months in a hill town like this one, Maya? I could take a sabbatical next semester. I'll compose and you ... Well, you could find something to do, couldn't you?"

She told him that she couldn't think of anything better than being with him in a hill town in Italy, but since she was teaching at two colleges, getting away for a whole semester would hardly be possible.

"My darling, I don't want you to waste your talents on those part-time, low-paying jobs. They're simply exploiting you, as you know! I want us to be together! You'll come to San Diego. We'll get married. Then we'll travel. And then ... if you want to teach, if you say you must, then we'll find a place. But, who knows, perhaps you'll want to do something else?"

"Like what?"

"Like looking after your old, decrepit, exhausted, good-for-nothing Aleshenka. How's that for a life goal? By the way, have I officially proposed to you? I can't remember."

"You can't remember?"

Al suddenly dropped to one knee.

"Well, here it is. I would love to push up daisies with you. What would you say to that, my Maya?"

"To do what?"

"Just say 'yes' or 'no'!"

"Of course 'no!' I don't want to push up daisies with anybody! I want to make love...here, in the woods!"

Al stood up and brushed the dirt from the knee of his pants.

"First you break my heart with your refusal, then you want to make love? Fine, I'll marry your mother instead. She and I got along just fine playing Mozart for four hands."

"Okay, okay! Try me again before marrying my mother! Propose, but do come up with something better this time."

"Let's see. Hmm. Can you milk a kicking cow?"

"My God! Will I ever get a normal, sweet proposal, asking for my hand and heart or whatever you're supposed to ask for?"

"That's the way they used to propose in County Sligo where my mother's family comes from. An Irish peasant girl was supposed to be hard working. If she couldn't milk a kicking cow, then ... "

"County Sligo? Isn't that where Yeats spent his childhood?"

"You do know a thing or two, don't you?"

Al was taken with the idea of buying a house somewhere in Umbria or Tuscany and so they spent the next couple of days driving around and looking at properties. And then, as planned, they departed for Switzerland. Al wanted to introduce her to his Swiss relatives and especially to his daughter, who worked for the United Nations in Geneva.

His relatives turned out to be ordinary farmers, kind and simple people who welcomed her with open hearts.

But it was Al's daughter with whom she made an immediate connection, perhaps a rare thing between a grown-up woman and her would-be stepmother. They walked and talked as if they had always known each other, understanding by half-word and half-look.

6

Maya received a prenuptial gift from her fiancé. As a memento of their Italian trip, he gave her a signed score of the symphony he had conducted at the Basilica di Santa Cecilia. His future mother-in-law received a copy of the original manuscript of Mozart's early minuets.

Maya's relocation to the United States would require paper work, but Al urged her to come to San Diego where he lived, without delay. Their wedding would be a simple one without much ado. He was in the middle of work on a new composition and the interruption was unwelcome.

She had visited him in San Diego before. His house in La Jolla, Spanish Revival style with a red terracotta-tile roof, was sheltered by tall eucalyptus trees and jacaranda covered with purple blossoms in the spring. A round tower on one side of the house served as a studio with a separate entrance.

The living room was Spartan, with only a few pieces of furniture: an antique chest and chairs with carved Gothic backs around an old oak table. The only colour was provided by a large Persian rug in the center of the dark tile floor. The room's austere simplicity reminded her of a Vermeer interior. There was something abstract, lacking any sign of domestic coziness, about the space. But the very abstractness of it, she thought, suited the abstract art of music and its devotee: the benevolent, but remote genius whose sanctuary it was.

She never asked to see the studio, but she did wonder what kind of musical instruments he kept there, since there weren't any in the main part of the house.

He had a violin, a flute, and a Steinway baby grand in the studio, he explained, all of which he rarely used. He composed in his head, with a pencil and the evolving score in front of him. He could hear each instrument separately, or all of them together the way they would sound when played by an orchestra. That ability seemed nothing short of miraculous to her.

7

When one day they finally sat down to make a list of guests for their wedding, Al suddenly remembered that he had a department meeting at the university. He apologized, changed, and soon was gone.

She looked at his scribbles at the top of a sheet of paper and at the abandoned pencil still warm from his fingers. The house suddenly felt alien to her—she didn't want to be there alone. She sat still for a moment and then went outside.

Small palm trees around the courtyard responded to the light breeze with a dry whisper, as if fingering their narrow leaves like musical instruments. The eucalyptuses produced an unfamiliar medicinal smell. She touched the white center of a bougainvillea flower surrounded by waxy scarlet bracts to make sure it was alive, was real and not cut out of paper. The sun was approaching its zenith and the heat soon drove her back into the house.

Sulking is not good, she told herself. She should do something useful—make borscht, for example. When Aleshenka came back he would appreciate her efforts.

Darkness fell, but she was still alone. When the heat finally passed, she opened a window to get fresh air from the ocean. And then she heard the faint sounds of a violin in the tower. He must have gone straight to his studio without checking on her first. She sat in the darkness with the lights turned off, listening, waiting. He finally returned to the house around nine. She got up to turn on the lights. "No, no, please leave it that way," he said. "I'm tired."

Without touching the borscht in the darkness, he went to his bedroom and closed the door. For some time she sat in the dark, afraid to move. By the time she finally entered the bedroom he was already asleep.

The pencil and paper for the wedding guest list lay on the table for one more day and then it disappeared.

The hot, monotonous days dragged on like molasses. Al always returned from work late, too tired to talk. One evening after he got back she decided to cheer him up with some music. Out of his small collection of CDs (she was surprised at how small it actually was) she chose one with Beethoven sonatas. He looked at her in utter horror, and she immediately turned it off.

The next morning, having nothing else to do, she thought she would go to the beach for a swim. The surf was calm with low waves fringed with foam. Excited to see the ocean, to taste it, to feel its power, she stepped into the water. It was her element, the water. The glittering infinity embraced her, and she felt great excitement in her body, similar to what she felt in Al's now melancholy presence. But here she didn't have to restrain herself, to scale it down, the way she did with him. She abandoned herself to the waves, and when they filled her mouth with a bitter salt taste, that too felt good. That too was happiness and life.

She swam with powerful, emphatic strokes, as if Al were there and could see what a good swimmer she was, what a good body she had. Feeling the elasticity and strength of her muscles, she kept charging forward. When she finally looked around, the figures on the beach seemed tiny. She immediately turned and tried to swim back with smaller strokes to conserve her energy. But the harder she tried, the less progress she seemed to make. She was beginning to lose her strength but didn't want to admit what she already knew. The ocean held her in its grip. It wouldn't let her move forward even an inch.

"Lucky I saw you," said the lifeguard who pulled her out of the water into his inflatable raft. "You were caught in a rip tide. People have drowned here."

Al's only reaction afterward was, "Why such recklessness when we have a swimming pool here?" The way he said it made her heart sink.

She decided not to mention her later visit to the zoo alone. It could have sounded childish, perhaps even silly. The last time she had been to the San Diego zoo was when her children were young. But now, when she didn't know what to do with herself, the famous zoo was as good a place as any to pass the time. And who could say if she would ever return to San Diego again. Once that idea rose to the surface of her consciousness, her stomach churned and she started to feel sorry for herself.

The only animals at the zoo that really interested her were the primates, those caricatures of human beings. Everything we humans do in secret—picking our noses, scratching ourselves, copulating—they do in the open, and that's what makes them look both obscene and ridiculous.

The primate enclosures were empty, except for two shaggy chimps, a mother and a baby. The mother had climbed onto a boulder, several inches away from a wall. Facing it, she froze in complete stillness, her hairy arms dangling inertly beside her. That strange behavior reminded Maya of the way children were punished for the slightest infraction when she was little by making them stand facing the wall for an hour or more.

Some mysterious, seemingly random force that governed her life had brought her to the zoo, to the chimpanzee display, to show her that she too was now staring at a wall. She, too had reached a dead end. If that was so, she would leave San Diego and stop humiliating herself.

Just as that thought was passing through her mind, the mother chimp slowly, with a kind of human awkwardness, got down from the bolder and let her baby take her place. Now the baby stood in the same position, facing the wall. What was going on? What was the meaning of that odd ritual?

Suddenly it dawned on her. The only place providing any relief from the scorching heat was the shade provided by the wall. The mother had been cooling herself and now was letting her baby do the same.

Just how that gesture of maternal love was translated into hope for herself, Maya didn't know, but somehow it had been. No, not all was lost! What she needed was to have a frank, open conversation with Aleshenka. She would be compassionate. She would ask him what was worrying him, why he seemed so unhappy, when only recently they had both been so confident about their future together. If he had concerns, he would be relieved to find out how patient and understanding she was. She didn't want to rush him into anything. It actually made sense to wait a little longer. They weren't young, and both had left behind failed marriages and lived by themselves for many years, forming solitary habits. Once reassured, Aleshenka would relax and the bliss of Panicale would return to them in San Diego.

8

Having made her decision, she cheered up. As she walked around the house she hummed merry tunes and smiled to show Al how light-hearted she could be in spite of their mysterious, but certainly temporary difficulties. No doom and gloom there. She would make good use of her free time. She would take charge of the kitchen, cook nice meals, give him a sense of real home life when he came back from work. She even danced a little around the stove while cooking, all the while waiting for the moment when they could talk.

But the moment never came.

During the day Al was at the university, and when he got home he would lock himself in his studio. Her lonely dinners with her as the only consumer of her elaborate concoctions were followed by equally lonely nights. Al would fall asleep complaining of exhaustion, while she lay next to him staring at diffuse shafts of light moving across the ceiling. She didn't know what the source of that light was, but it illuminated Al's sleeping face, pale and solemn. It fell on his long, thick eyelashes, unusual in a man and even more so in a man in his fifties.

And so it continued. In spite of her patient waiting, the key to the closed door was never offered. She decided to look for it on her own.

Patiently, she retraced their steps in time, hoping to

locate the moment when the estrangement began. What had she said or done that had suddenly turned him away from her? Coming from different cultures, could it be that they had no common frame of reference? But that hadn't seemed to bother him in the past. So why now? And doesn't love conquer all?

The phone call from a woman who had been after him for a long time, as he told her? Could that have been it? Whenever he went to Iowa to visit his sister, that woman, brash, coarse, illiterate (his own description of her), and a friend of his sister's, would insist on meeting him at the airport and on carrying his suitcase. According to Al, she owned a laundromat and her son was in prison. She had turned herself into a real nuisance, he said.

No, of course that woman had nothing to do with it.

What was it, then? Had she said something wrong that offended him? Some stupid remark that he had taken personally? She couldn't think of anything, except for a dinner party at the home of his friends Richard and Gail. While cutting up some asparagus, Richard, a musicologist, had asked her what she thought of a performance they had all gone to two weeks before. It was an open-air concert with two full orchestras on two makeshift stages placed next to each other, performing two different pieces simultaneously with two conductors, one being Al and the other a guest from Japan.

No, she said, she hadn't liked it at all. "The truth is I can't imagine anybody else liking it either, if they're honest about it."

In that exemplary home, among all those refined people, her words may have seemed crass. Nobody there talked like that. She paused, realizing that she had gone too far. "Well, maybe as a musical experiment, it had some value."

Richard replied, "I wouldn't be so hard on it, or on Al, who organized the event. It was an experiment, as you rightly noted, and without experimentation, modern classical music will be kaput, will stop evolving. To achieve something great, you need to expand your consciousness, you need to get outside your box. Often you may need to be shaken out of it, because we're all creatures of habit. Too often we use clichés to express ourselves, as I'm sure you'll agree ...

"Are you familiar with John Cage's *4'33"*? That too seemed strange, even unthinkable, when it was composed in 1952. Now it's accepted as his most famous work. Never heard of it? Let me explain ... Four minutes and thirty-three seconds. It's not a random number. There's a significance to it, but we won't go into it now. Anyway, the musicians are on stage the entire time, but they don't play any music. But they are there with their instruments. You're watching them as you usually do during a concert, but now you listen not to them but with them. And that tiny semantic shift opens up a whole new world: not 'to' but 'with.'"

"Sorry, I'm not getting it. Listen to what, if there's no music?"

"You're listening to the symphony of life, and it, the symphony of life, becomes your most visceral, most primal, and, ultimately, your most cherished experience. You pay attention to sounds that in the past your brain would automatically have shut out, but now, through that active listening to silence ... Well, it's not really silence, is it? I mean, once you've activated the process of listening without arbitrarily assigning a hierarchy to the sounds, it becomes transformative. In simple terms, Cage forces you to abandon your expectations and recondition your brain. You hear some coughing in the audience. People usually try to suppress it, but now, they're awakened and freed. They're wondering what's going on and naturally they cough even more. Then you become aware of the traffic outside, cars honking. That too has its own beauty. Then you hear the chairs being pushed back after the musicians finish and get up to take a bow—you have embraced it all! Cage has liberated you from your *cage*, so to speak. He has finally allowed you to live! You have gone from to ivory tower to the symphony of life ... See?"

She should have nodded in agreement, but instead she said, "Why do I need to buy tickets to a concert hall to listen to traffic noise, when I can simply stand on any street corner for that?"

Did Al hear her? And decide that she was a conventional snob, a philistine? He was standing a distance away from them near a sliding glass door that faced the garden. Rows of flowerpots flanked the steps that came up to the door and, studded with similar flowers, continued into the living room. The arrangement united the indoor and outdoor spaces into one, creating the illusion of an endless garden, and she thought it would be nice to suggest something like that to Alesha for his house after she had moved in.

He hadn't turned around, so it may be that he didn't hear her but was preoccupied with his own thoughts, as he so often was.

9

He had already switched the key from major to minor and back again several times, so that it remained ambiguous right through to the final bars. Freakish and frantic. Shostakovich had done the same thing before him in his String Quartet No.12. Quoting the great Russian, quoting somebody else? Nothing wrong with that. But too many of his recent compositions had either revamped his own earlier ones or had borrowed from other composers, and that was a problem. He had run out of ideas and he knew it. They—the collective "they" of international connoisseurs and snooping critics—so far, they hadn't sniffed it out. But sooner or later, they would. Look! The emperor is naked. Look, he's withered away! He's finished! Finished at fifty-seven.

"Maya understands little of what I'm doing, so she admires me. Those enraptured eyes ... The imposter is going to deliver a glamorous world on a golden plate. I should disabuse her of her illusion. But how? I've tried to downplay it, tried to distance myself from it and refer to it ironically. But she's implacable. She's made an effigy of me, put me on a pedestal, and now keeps holding me there with both hands. Tiptoeing around so she won't disturb me. Thinking I won't hear! I, who can hear every scrap of sound! What tension, what anguish!

"Not to mention the lights. Sitting there by herself in the dark like a nun doing penance. Do I begrudge her the electricity?

"And then her moods: from low to high in a split second! Is she bipolar and I failed to notice? That dress she put on the other day, the same one she was wearing in the Basilica di Santa Cecilia. A 'subtle' nod to our happier times in Italy? Dancing, prancing in front of me ... What a tacky performance that was! I won't deny it: we did have some happy moments in Panicale. Because I did well in Rome and then in Bari, that's why. And yes, she looked lovely, everybody noticed, and I was touched...Thank God, there was little of her 'high-brow' chatter there. Poor thing, she somehow feels compelled to do it when she wants to impress me, 'to live up to me' as she once put it.

"But in the Panicale groves, she let go of her pretensions. And she looked pretty. I thought I was in love ... But here? She doesn't belong here, that much is clear. Is it my fault? Hers? It's nobody's.

"But I said that I loved her, didn't I? I thought I loved her there in the groves of Panicale. And if I did, what happened to my love? What happens to all our loves? If I were God, I could answer that question. Yes, that's it. Where is God? I've lost the sense of his presence, and then ... And then God abandoned me. I can't compose any more. He has left me.

"She came late into my life. Had we both been younger, had we met when I was at the height of my abilities, would things have been any different? Who can say?

"This section in the first movement that I've been working on for weeks is junk. I used to be able to compose a symphony in a month.

"Compose? It always felt like it was already there, waiting for me. That I was merely a conduit, a channel through which God's energy, the energy of the universe, was flowing. All I had to do was to submit myself. To listen humbly, patiently, and then write it down as quickly as possible while it was still there, and frequently without any corrections. The fever, the ardor, the exuberance of those fourteen-hour workdays when I could go without food, and sleep, my enemy, seemed merely a waste of time ...

"But have I forgotten what would happen afterwards? The despondency, the overwhelming sadness that was the price I paid for my triumphs. Bach, Mozart, Telemann, they didn't waste a moment. They would immediately get to work on their next piece, and then on the next, and then on the one after that.

"But not me. I would suck my paw, feeling totally spent, empty, vacant. In the fragile days that followed, I would yearn for a woman's body. Her softness against my chest. Her sleepy sweet voice—the way they talk in bed, pretending to be little girls before they fall asleep.

"Yes, I wanted a wife then, and I took one, the future

mother of Fiona. Ultimately, it didn't work between two musicians, both young and full of ambition as we were. But now, in my 'sunset years', do I really need a wife? I don't know any more.

"What I want is a simple, ordinary woman who will stand by me, a silent, unquestioning presence when I'm finished with a day of composing, someone who will look after my home and free me from chores, which consume so much of my time right now.

"But if I go ahead with Maya and uproot her, I will have to take care of her, and I can't afford that! I can't afford the time. I still have many irons in the fire. I'll compose and conduct and perform and submit to music again, the way I've always done, humbly yet ecstatically, akin to surrendering to a woman, a simple, strong, earth-bound, sensual woman, with an eager body that will ease me out of my shell, free me from my ego, just as music has always done.

"And Maya? Admit it. She isn't that woman. She has a nice body but somehow her ways leave me cold. Why? I don't know. What difference does it make? I'm a coward! A cad! I don't even have the heart to be honest with her. But I don't want to hurt her! I'll do everything I can not to hurt her! But how do you break such news to a woman in love? I mean, I do like her ... I'll search for help. I'll search for God. I'll search for faith."

He buried his head in his hands trying to subdue the sob that suddenly escaped his throat. It was already close to midnight when he finally returned from his studio to his dark, mute house.

10

The psychologist Al insisted they see, a big, burly black man with an engaging smile, extended his arms as if he wanted to embrace them: "You guys love each other! Look at you!"

According to the psychologist, Al's problem was his fear of commitment.

"You have to overcome your fear. my friend—I hope to be invited to your wedding! In the meantime, you, Maya, you will have to give your fiancé some time. Are you ready for that?"

She couldn't help smiling back at that jovial, bear-like man and promised to make the best use of his advice.

When later that evening she told Al that she had already bought a return ticket home, he was visibly upset. At the airport, he looked disoriented, dazed. Their love would prevail, he said. He just had to find the path he had temporarily lost. Just before she said her final good-bye, he pressed an envelope into her hand.

She flew from San Diego to Toronto so she could visit a sick friend and then took the train home to Montréal the next day. Sitting by the window, she gazed apathetically out at the wintry landscape running backwards. She hadn't had the courage to open Al's envelope on the plane, but now, finally, she did.

There was a check in it for $5,000 and a note: "I hope the time of deep introspection we both need will show us a path to happiness and contentment. With much love, Albrecht."

She put the note back in the envelope. She didn't realize that the cheque had slipped out onto the floor until a moment later when she lifted her eyes to see a short man in a smart suit standing next to her with the check in his hand.

"You're spreading your fortune around, miss," he said, smiling. He introduced himself as Ralph Gartenberg and asked if he could take the empty seat beside her. He talked fast, giggling at his own jokes. It seemed utterly strange to her that anybody could find anything funny about this world. When they got off the train, he offered to help with her suitcase. It turned out that they were almost neighbors. He lived in Côte Saint-Luc, two blocks from her home.

That spring, to her complete surprise, she received a letter from Al's daughter. Fiona reminisced about the good time and conversations they had had in Geneva. She expressed her sincere regrets that Maya's marriage to her father had fallen through and added that her father had recently married a woman from Iowa, a friend of his sister's. Fiona expressed great concern about her father. She thought that the couple was poorly matched and that her father was unhappy. She wished Maya well and invited her to visit her in Geneva if she was ever in Europe.

11

When, almost two years after those events, I moved from Montréal to Vancouver, Ralph had long disappeared from my horizon. But one day I picked up the phone and heard his voice. He was calling from Vancouver. "The Space Agency people will now have to come to talk to me here. I've moved my meetings to Vancouver, hee-hee!" he said with his familiar self-satisfied chuckle.

When, after dinner in the rotating restaurant, we went down to his room, Ralph said, "Do you like your present? I wanted to get you some roses too to put in the vase, but I came here straight from the airport. Tomorrow, when we go for a walk, I'll get you some good ones. Do you think the flower shops are open on Sunday?"

"I'm actually not sure about tomorrow. Not sure about a walk in Stanley Park with you."

"Fine. You don't have to if it makes you so unhappy. Just don't be angry with me, Maya."

"I'm not angry. I feel sorry for you ... "

"Sorry? Well, don't! It only makes things worse. Just so that you know ... If you really insist on talking about it again ... I hate myself for what I've been doing to you and my wife. I'm an idiot, completely screwed up! I never told you, or maybe I did, but Esther is very unhappy. She senses that I've changed. In a way, she's like you: vulnerable, unsure of herself ... And she needs me. I'm her fortress. No decision is ever made without me. My father taught me to be a mensch, to protect my family, and I always have.

"But with you, I don't know what happened to me. All I know is that I love you, the way I have never loved any other woman in my life. When I was in Toronto I missed you terribly, I counted the days till I was back in Montréal again and could call you, hear your voice ... I came to Vancouver to see you. I had no other reason. You understand? No other reason at all!"

He paused. I sat at the edge of the sofa without moving.

"But listen. If you say now that you never want to see me again, if you really say that, I'll disappear. I promise. Just say it. Don't say you pity me. Don't tell me I'm a good person. Don't say you're grateful for my help. Say what you really feel: that I'm a nuisance, that you want to be rid of me. Say that all I'm doing is hurting you. Say it, say it, and I'll never bother you again!"

He turned away from me, his voice breaking. "I'm a wreck. I'm not myself any more. But I'll keep my word."

"I never meant you or your family any harm, you know that," I whispered, trying to hold back my tears.

"Yes, I know. And I respect that. And, yes, I'll keep my word. But if you want me to have any kind of peace in the future, promise me one thing: if you're ever in trouble or you need anything at all, you'll let me know. I'll find a way. Promise?"

"Yes ... "

"Oh, Maya, my darling, my little girl! Sit next for me

for a moment. Like that ...You have such smooth hands ... wonderful skin ... Hug me. Let me kiss you. Our first and our last."

I felt his quick tongue searching in my mouth, and for a moment I lost my breath.

"Take it off. Take off your bra. You don't need any of that. There. Oh, you smell so good!"

"I'm cold. What are you doing?"

"Cold? But it's stifling hot in here."

He quickly pulled the blanket off one side of the bed, pulled me over, and covered me with a sheet.

"Better now? Let me touch your face, just your face ... Your neck, there, there...Your breast is so smooth."

"Ah, it hurts! My breasts hurt ... "

"Hurt? I hardly touched them. I'll be gentle."

"The light, turn it off. It's in my eyes."

"No. I want to see you. I want to see your body. Let me kiss your nipple."

"Ow, it hurts!"

"But I'm not doing anything. Your nipples are erect: you're excited ... "

"No-o-o! My nipples are scared!"

"What do you mean, scared? Nipples don't get scared. There, I'll calm them down, you poor little thing, so sensitive. Now what? Are you having your period? Is that why you're so jumpy?"

"No, it's ten days from now, but it already hurts."

"Your ears aren't hurting, are they? Give me this little snail, so perfectly shaped. You're my sensitive princess on a pea. That's why I love you! Now, your armpit. Your tummy. Your belly button. Oh, my sweet girl, my darling ... I want to do all kinds of things to you. And I will."

"Like what?"

"You'll see. Where's your lipstick? You had lipstick somewhere."

"My lipstick? What for?"

"Just tell me where you put it."

He rolled over to the edge of the bed, reached for my purse on the bed table, and got the lipstick out. Then he drew scarlet circles around each nipple.

"Now we'll know where it hurts, so we don't touch it. We're just going to drink milk out of these pink buttons. Imagine that I'm your baby!"

"Good God! You're insane!"

"Oh, that tastes good. Now I've got you!" he whispered, drawing horizontal lines across my belly, my inner thighs, then crisscrossing them with vertical lines.

"Oh stop it! What are you doing?! You're making a terrible mess!"

"Don't worry, they'll wash the sheets. It's their job."

"It's like my whole body is bleeding!"

"No. You're not bleeding now, as you told me. You're being jailed. Locked behind red bars. That's where I'll keep you. You're mine now, mine! Spread your legs."

"N-o-o!"

"Oh, yes! You're going to do what I say. This last time. You're so tight inside. There! You're going to have a real man now, my princess."

"But you're hurting me!"

"If it hurts you, it hurts me too, don't you know? It hurts us both. We're now one. You're just out of practice, darling. But we'll take care of that. With such a body you need a man. You're going to have a man every goddamn night now. Me!"

"Oh, stop talking ...What gibberish ... Stop it!"

"I always talk when I'm ... when I make love ...Whether you want it or not, you're going to have a real man now. And then you'll be happy! I'll finally make you happy, you'll see. You'll love it. You've got to love it! There, there!"

"I'm telling you it hurts!"

"That's all right. You can take it from Ralph. Not going to be long. Once, just once. Do you have any cream or something?"

"What? What are you talking about?!"

"You never thought it would come to this, did you, my innocent girl! Then lipstick will have to do. Bear with me. You just have to take it. See, it's better now. That's a good girl! It doesn't hurt now, does, it? Oh, that was beautiful ... You feel so good. I love you! Love you, love you. Oh my God, Maya!"

"Don't pull away from me, my sweet girl. I'm not finished! I've been dreaming about it, do you know how long?

Do you? Let me rest for ten minutes. Oh, my God, what have I done to you?"

He began to mumble as his voice drifted away into sleep.

His foot twitched as he fell asleep. That's how it ends: in a dance of death.

I separated myself from his sweaty, limp body by rolling up the edge of the blanket and placing it between us. He was lying on his side with the light from the lamp on his bare shoulder and its tufts of curly, half-grey hair, a shoulder that, without the padding of his suit jacket, looked as small and vulnerable as that of a child. I lay there lead-heavy, listening as his breathing turn into snoring, with a thin whistle at the end of each exhalation

There was a sound of a siren. The city was never quiet. A police car or an ambulance? Somebody having a heart attack? A stroke? Somebody dying? They'll admit him and start filling out the forms, but it will be too late. The person will die. They'll all die just as I was dying now.

No, I wasn't going to die. I would get up, wash the lipstick off, and leave. An easy thing to do. There were always taxis waiting in front. I would just get up. That's all I needed to do.

But I couldn't. I couldn't move even my pinky, let alone wash. I would wash at home and for now just try to get up. Slowly, quietly, one leg out of the bed at a time. Bra? No need for it. I put it my purse. Panties and hose? It's not that cold, I could manage without them. The disgusting taste in my mouth? My parched lips? That musky smell? All because I was there in that awful place. As soon as I got home, I would forget all about it. Forever. As if it had never happened. Ever!

But it had happened. That's why I was dying. I was dying, but at least he had stopped twitching, thank God. He wouldn't wake up now. I could use the corner of the sheet to wipe off the lipstick and disappear. He would be upset when he woke up. He loves me. Be fair to him. Don't hate him. Pity him. And then I started to fall asleep myself. The sound of another ambulance, and then of a third driving right up to the hotel. Somebody was dying. They were all dying there on the other side of the walls, and it was my fault.

"What's going on? What's that sound?" Ralph sat up in bed, instantly alert as if he hadn't been snoring just a second ago. "Are you all right?" His hand reached for me.

"Couldn't be any better," I replied without looking at him.

"A fire alarm! Get up, Maya. Get dressed! Quick! It's serious. The hotel's on fire! We have to get out. Get up, Maya! Get up!"

Without losing his composure, he was dressed in a minute, ready to flee with his briefcase already in hand.

"We won't take the elevator but use the stairs all the way down. Don't panic! It's only fifteen floors. And I'm with you. Please don't panic! We'll be just fine!"

Suddenly I felt a rush of angry, vindictive energy.

Ordering me around as if I were his spoiled, helpless wife!
How poorly did he know me! I wasn't like her at all! Ha-ha!
Let him keep her on the short leash of his nauseating care, not
me!

"Who's panicking?" I shouted as I ran down the stairs,
skipping steps for the sheer joy of it. "What is there to panic
about?! It's fun! Can't you see how much fun it is?"

I didn't give a damn about the fire or anything else. Let
the hotel and the world with it go up in flames. I was alive!
Boom, boom, alive!

"Wait! Not so fast! You're scared. Don't panic! It will
be fine!"

A confused crowd, their faces creased from sleep, some
still in their pajamas, had gathered outside the hotel entrance.
Nobody talked or asked questions. It was drizzling. A grey,
puny day was about to emerge from its shell.

We never found out what happened. Not wanting to
frighten their clientele, the hotel staff assured the crowd that it
was quite safe to go back inside. Nothing had happened at the
Empire Landmark Hotel on that particular day. Nothing at all.

"In your case, I think it will better to see your family
physician," said a young female doctor at the walk-in clinic.

"I don't have one," I lied.

"Is this your first pregnancy?"

"I have two grown children."

"Well, that will make it easier. Still, I'm sure you're

aware that a pregnancy at forty-six could be risky for the baby and the mother. You'll have to give yourself plenty of rest."

"There isn't going to be a baby. Do you need me to sign any forms?"

12

Twenty years latter Vancouver had changed beyond all recognition. The cost of land had driven retail shops into the remote suburbs, with the city's malls, gas stations, and bookstalls replaced by expensive condominiums.

My long cherished desire for the Empire Landmark Hotel to vanish from the face of the earth was finally granted. But it didn't go up in flames. Instead, workers surgically removed each floor, starting with the rotating restaurant on the forty-second, going all the way down to the fifteenth, and then down to very foundation. The hotel was in a densely populated area and jets of water were continuously sprayed over its concrete and steel carcass until the demolition was complete.

Not long ago I went back to Montréal for a book launch. My sixth book had just come out. To my relief, the city's European flavor remained intact. Solid old grey stone houses with gables, garrets, ornate balconies, and staircases winding along their facades gave the urban center a feeling of permanence, of established life and unbroken tradition. I stayed with a friend in Côte Saint-Luc, where I had lived so many years before.

One afternoon by a vegetable stand, I noticed an wizened old man, his shaggy beard and unkempt hair rippling in the wind. Leaning heavily on his cane, he was bent over a cardboard box of watermelons. A small line of customers watched patiently as he awkwardly, with one hand, turned over the watermelons, trying to find one he would be able to lift. His left arm hung inertly from his drooping left shoulder, obviously of little use to him. He moved about in worn-out sandals that exposed his dirty, unclipped toenails.

"These are too big for me to handle. Have you got anything smaller?" he asked the vendor. The old man's voice sounded vaguely familiar, but I couldn't place it. I moved closer. The rank smell of his old, unwashed body enveloped me. His watery eyes with puffy bags gave me a tired, perfunctory glance.

"Ralph?" I said, hoping I was mistaken but knowing with certainty that that crooked form belonged to none other than Ralph Gartenberg. "You don't recognize me, do you. It's Maya."

"Maya?" He looked me over again. "Is that you? Ah. How we have all changed. You were much slimmer then, I remember. Yes, we all change. . ."

"What are you doing here?"

"Buying a watermelon, as you see."

"I mean, do you live in Montréal now?"

"Yes, in Côte Saint-Luc. Where I've always lived."

"Your family ultimately moved to Montréal?"

"No, they stayed behind. I moved."

I watched him as he finally found a small watermelon, paid for it, managed to slip it into the canvas tote he was carrying, and then tried, with his right hand, to hang the tote from his right shoulder.

"Let me help you, Ralph."

"No need," he brusquely replied. After several tries he succeeded, and then slowly, dragging his left foot, he limped away.

I followed him, unwilling to let him go.

"We haven't seen each other for what? Twenty years or more? Your children ... and mine are all adults now ... How are yours doing, by the way?"

"My children haven't stayed in touch with me, so I can't answer that question."

"Oh? I'm so sorry to hear that."

"So am I. Good-by, Maya."

"No, wait, wait. Can I do something for you? Help you in any way?"

He stopped, shifted the tote, and then for the first time our eyes met.

"No, you can't help me, Maya." He paused. "So far, I've been able to manage on my own."

"Oh, I see ... Uh. Uh. I suppose you're retired now. But your health seems to have deteriorated," I said, carefully stating the obvious. "Somebody must be helping you. I hope Esther is in good health?"

"You remember my wife's name, huh? Didn't I tell you a minute ago that Esther doesn't live in Montréal? She divorced me many years ago."

"Esther ... divorced you? How can that be?"

"Anything is possible in this world, as you can see."

"Forgive me for asking, but why? What was the reason?"

"You really need to know? The law of entropy. She found out about you."

"But ... I didn't ... Since the hotel fire we haven't been in touch."

"That's true. But after you left, I couldn't really...I mean I wasn't coping very well, especially the first year. Esther was my closest friend, the mother of my children. I couldn't deceive her anymore. So I told her."

"But it's been years! There was really nothing between us. Besides, people forgive each other. And reconcile."

"Oh, yes. She forgave me. And we reconciled. But she said that I should be free to love whomever I wanted. Good-bye, Maya. I really need to go now."

He hobbled away, dragging his left foot and raising his right shoulder to keep the tote from slipping off.

It was June and the cottonwoods were shedding their summer "snow" in fluffy tufts. The pods rolled across the pavement, sticking in every crack in the asphalt and clogging the gutters. Playfully, as if engaged in some game, they whirled under the wheels of cars, whirled in a wild *farandole* in front of white Apollo in the form, perhaps, of a dilapidated violin and a faded manuscript ...

Ralph stopped for a moment, hit a snow-tuft with his cane, and continued on his way.

Philosophy Lessons

For Sasha
when he was little

1

When I was a student reading German metaphysics, I came
across the folio of an early fifteenth-century Marburg alchemist
and physician named Balthasar von Reinstüsser. Balthasar
had spent his life searching for an explanation of that strange
phenomenon, the human heart. What force, he asked, sets in
motion that tiny lump of flesh while it is still in the womb?
What makes the fetus's newly formed heart produce its first
beat and begin the long journey that will end only with its
death? In Balthasar's view, Divine Providence had started the
heart beating the same way that a clockmaker sets a pendulum
in motion with a tap or a nudge. But exactly how did that
happen? With a touch of God's finger? A sudden descent of
divine inspiration? Or was the sheer energy of Divine Reason
enough by itself to give new life its impetus? The alchemist
believed that in order to respond to God's call, to God's
command, the new heart needs be tender and yielding, exactly
the kind of heart that everybody is born with.

Many years later I found in a medical treatise an
answer to the alchemist's question. The delicate nature of
its tissue is necessary for the heart to react easily to tiny
electrical impulses, a fact that may also make it responsive to
electromagnetic or even sonic effects, either of those a possible
stimulus for the first beat. And in the same way, a strong
enough external physical impact may be enough for the heart

to stop beating. Thus, if the blow of a ball or a stone should happen to coincide with the amplitude of the heart's own rhythm, then the heart might stop beating. Could an emotional trauma have the same effect as a physical one, unexpectedly leading to death?

I'm now seventy-six and just as curious about things as I ever was. I still like to learn, even though the names of books and their authors may sometimes slip away. And I often forget what I've read, which for me is the most distressing part. I suppose I can still pun the way I used to and tell a funny story to the point—if there were somebody to tell it to, that is. As it happens, my late wife, Priscilla, was never bothered by her lapses of memory, which were much more pronounced than my own.

Half-in-jest, I comfort myself with the idea that my brain is trying to return to Aristotle's *tabula rasa*, to its primordial state of pure potentiality, when all the neural pathways were still uncluttered and it was possible to inscribe.

But what exactly at this point, what fresh insights could I inscribe on my own aged wax tablet? Might it be (as I follow my own logic) that obliviousness to the physical world is a necessary step for recovering the true knowledge that, as Plato supposed, we had in full measure before we were born? The knowledge that will be revealed to us once again after we die? "If no pure knowledge is possible in the company of the body, then either it is completely impossible to acquire it, or is possible only after death," Socrates said in the *Phaedo* in the days before taking his life.

I have no doubt that my memory got worse after I retired, and I'm sorry that I ever did. The college where I taught philosophy for nearly forty years would have let me stay on. Of course, teaching ancient philosophers to eighteen-year-old ninnies, most of them anyway, was an ungrateful business. Rarely in recent years did they put down their electronic devices long enough to gaze in my direction. Standing before them, I often felt like some disinterred fuddy-duddy whose time had long since passed and whose interests had no connection at all to their young lives. If you think I'm grousing like an old codger, wait until you reach my age.

Although I'm no great fan of contemporary technology, I did consult the Internet about my memory lapses. Let's suppose, some neurologist wrote there, that you completely forget about a medical appointment. They call to remind you. Glasses, wallet, keys, a spare battery for your hearing aid, all of that finally stuffed into your pockets, you hurry out the door. Fine. But now suppose that you hang up and stay put, since the call itself is something that you're no longer aware of. The first scenario is part of the normal aging process. The second is the decline, the death in life, of Alzheimer's.

If I am to trust the good Internet doctor, I really have nothing to worry about. All the same, I decided to make my life a little easier by writing notes to myself about one thing and another.

Now before going to the store, I jot down whatever

I need—no more than a few items, usually, since I don't eat much. I never used to rely on shopping lists, regarding people who wander through supermarkets with slips of paper in their hands as feeble-minded at best. My prejudices are strong, and I'm still reluctant to get out my own slip of paper. But usually a finger's touch in my pocket is enough to boost my confidence. From grocery lists I've moved on to copying down for no special purpose fragments from books and articles that have caught my attention.

Recently, for example, I recorded the following. The thirteenth-century Holy Roman Emperor and King of Sicily and Jerusalem Frederick II was a man of insatiable but cruel scientific curiosity. He once ordered the complete isolation of several infants from any human speech to see if they would start speaking the language of Adam and Eve on their own, instead of using their parents' native tongue, be it Hebrew or Greek or Latin or Arabic or any of the other possibilities. He is also said to have had a man sealed inside a barrel to find out if his soul could be observed leaving the container after the poor victim had suffocated ...

As I was writing all that down, a light snow started to fall. Outside my study window, I could see snowflakes sliding down the shiny dark green leaves of the rhododendron next to our house. Years ago, Priss had planted a bush there that at the time scarcely reached my windowsill, although now it's a small tree. Priss loved the fluffy crimson spume of its flowers. But I find that bacchanal of colour excessive, and in its papery artificiality even the gorgeous inflorescence itself looks lifeless to me. The red maple growing behind the fence in our backyard is much more to my liking. It retains its modest rusty-brown leaves until the beginning of winter. Then they all seem to drop off at once. I enjoy the way they slowly spin in the air before settling on the driveway's damp surface with what look like open hands. The day it snowed, they were cold, and that made them curl their fingers like living hands—or so it seemed to me.

2

Ever since Priss died two years ago, I've felt in my dreams an exhilarating sense of liberation (we had tried to separate several times during our long life together). But as soon as I awake, a heavy boulder of guilt collapses on me, pressing down on my chest. The stillness of the empty rooms at night is a particular torment, and every morning I look for an excuse to get out of the house. I don't do volunteer work. I dislike clubs. So that usually means merely wandering around the city, something that also frees me from having to answer the phone. My old girlfriend, Brigid, calls several times a day. I'll hear her loud breathing for a moment, since she no longer bothers to leave messages, knowing that I rarely check them. Of course, I could just unplug the phone, but I don't, subconsciously hoping, I suppose, for an unexpected call, God knows from whom, or else for some bit of happy news, some unexpected joy. Need I add that the phone is almost always silent?

I've known Brigid for over thirty-five years, almost as long as I knew Priss. Our relationship is a moldy, ramshackle thing now. The quick, easy laughter and inner glow that attracted me to that red-haired, grey-eyed woman have vanished along with our youth. She's faded now and her flesh is starting to sag, and when her head is tipped at a certain angle, she looks amazingly like Priss. If I should ever happen to wake up in her bed (a complete impossibility), I would be met by the same slack, vacant look I never could get used to in Priss; the same shuffling slippers and complaints about being tired after a "hard" night; the same grumbling about high prices and the rudeness and vulgarity of life in our glass city, which have been metastasizing like an aggressive melanoma, and about the razing of beautiful old Victorian homes, the constant traffic jams from the endless street repair; and the tattoos disfiguring backs and arms and legs and, no doubt, other places too.

Priss suffered from migraines and couldn't tolerate the sun. Brigid suffers from nightmares and complains about the rain. I don't rule out that Priss found out about Brigid at some point (how could she not have in thirty-five years?), and it's even possible that the women met and, organizing a cabal of two, had a good deal of hearty giggling at my expense.

Although Priss eventually accepted my refusal to have children, the fact that she had to leave England when I was offered a job in Canada was something that she never could forgive. And because of me too, Brigid never got married. She hoped for my liberation, waiting for years in the wings, so it's not surprising that now she wants to be the sole manager of what remains of my life. Poor Brigid! That wish has zero chance of fulfillment!

My walks usually take me away from home for as much as three or four hours.

I make my way across rumbling Burrard Bridge, which connects Vancouver's business district on the peninsula with Kitsilano, where my house stands on a steep slope above English Bay. Across the bay to the left I can see the shoreline of Stanley Park and the dense, almost black stand of evergreens that occupies the peninsula's western tip.

There might seem to be no good reason for an old man with a walking stick (more for security than need) to be walking across that enormous bridge, but I'm stubborn. Although the bridge is defended on both sides with masses of steel (it was built in the 1930s), I still can't bring myself to look at the water far below. My gaze soars aloft to follow the bridge's heavy, dirty-yellow arches down to where they end on the north side in paired but strangely confused art-nouveau Roman sarcophagi with Egyptian wings. Bicycle riders, those sleek greyhounds, separated from the bridge traffic by large concrete blocks, seem to be the only people in Vancouver who actually care about their looks: nylon tights, bright jerseys and jackets, matching fingerless gloves. What a sharp contrast to the sloppy blouses, drab untucked-in oversize shirts, and khaki pants slipping off the hips of pedestrian bipeds. I regret that the greyhounds have started to abandon their old brightly colored, streamlined helmets, which reminded me of wing-footed Hermes, the ancient god of travelers and guide to the Underworld. The new helmets, dull-green round things of quasi-military design ... Well, whoever decreed them fashionable must have been nostalgic for WWII.

Ahead of me and on my left is the magnificent bluish-black mountain range that abuts the city in a continuous wall. It seems that I can reach out and almost touch the mountains, but that's obviously an illusion. From October to March, the mountains are often covered in fog. Sometimes it descends to hang in a wispy mantle over the Salish Sea. As if the mountains' feet were in the water and their heads in the air. Behind me, as I walk east, the Salish Sea gradually narrows into English Bay and then into the sleeve of the False Creek estuary. Huddled in the False Creek marina, yachts and powerboats gently sway, the narrow strips of water between them dark blue against their brilliant white.

Fifty years ago False Creek was the city's industrial edge, with a sawmill and narrow-gauge railway and loading yards extending along the northern flank. But all that's gone now. High-rise apartment buildings have taken its place, the asphalt surrounding them yielding here and there to sketched-in islets of grass. Concrete, glass, stainless steel. The skinny little trees planted around the buildings, each tree supported by a wooden brace, look like orphans against the modern architecture's cold sterility. I feel sorry for the trees planted on the roofs of high-rises. In a forest, tree roots '"talk" to each other, exchanging chemicals. They help their brothers in distress. It pains me to think of the solitude of roots of trees planted hundreds of meters above the ground.

Who lives in those high-rises, blank and glassy blue, like the vacant eyes of a dragonfly? They must be creatures with reticulated wings who are free of routine and domestic life. I see them flitting out onto the quayside individually, some jogging, some hurtling past on bikes or skates, with a few of the joggers pushing infants in three-wheeled strollers.

What is it that draws me to False Creek? After all, if I wanted to see English Bay and the Coast Mountains, I could go out the back gate of my house and down the path to the water for an unobstructed view. Perhaps it's the proximity of other people, the bustle I used to dislike but that has become such a welcome contrast to the atmosphere of my own home, to the mute clutter of it, now that Priss is no longer there.

Priss was superstitiously afraid of empty spaces, and over the course of our life together she gradually dragged into our home half of Main Street and its musty second-hand furniture shops. All the rooms (except for my study) are now crammed with chiffoniers, dressers, étagères with elaborate inlays, useless standing lamps, card tables with fake Tiffany lamps, Chinese jade figurines, little porcelain elephants on lace doilies, and similar junk. After Priss died, I considered getting rid of it all, but then I decided against it, afraid it would only aggravate my lingering guilt. When she was alive, I silently struggled against her whole being, so unlike my own. But now that the struggle has ended, I'm unable to find any peace with myself. Somehow I've been turned into some contrived, abstract creature akin to those denizens of the barren high-rises of False Creek and the quayside.

3

After the effort of the bridge crossing I need to rest. I continue east along my usual route past the moored yachts and powerboats until I come to my favorite bench facing the harbor. I take out of my jacket pocket a little chess set that I usually carry with me. There was a time when I could play against myself in my mind, but now I need to have a board and pieces.

Absorbed in the game, I didn't notice that a little boy had climbed up onto the bench beside me. He had evidently been watching me play for some time.

He looked to be around five or six. Curly chestnut hair framed the healthy glow of his round, dark-peach face and cherub's cheeks. His bright red lips, full like a girl's, kept twitching as if trying to keep from smiling. Taking a closer look, I realized that his face combined European and Asian features, with a small nose, dark, wide-spaced eyes, and prominent cheek bones. The combination of slightly slanted eyes and curly hair was unusual, but what was most striking about him wasn't that but something elusively tender, something aloofly affectionate in his demeanor. He told me that his name was Giovanni, and the Italian inflection only added to his mystery.

"Can I play too?" he finally got up the courage to ask.

"Do you really know how to?" I skeptically replied.

"My papa taught me. But we have a real chess set. Papa made it out of wood."

"This is a real chess set too, only it's small so I can carry it around in my pocket."

"Can I touch it?"

Giovanni picked a queen from the little board, carefully looked at it from every side, and then put it back. He examined the king the same way, and then evidently having satisfied himself that they were indeed real despite being small, he moved closer on the bench, sighed, and was silent.

"Are you Santa Claus?" he suddenly asked, looking at my face with a sly grin.

"Do I look like him?"

"You have a white beard and a cane just like Santa Claus. Can I touch the cane?"

He carefully examined my walking stick, which I had bought in India. He was especially intrigued by its intricately carved boxwood handle shaped like the head of a snake.

"Can it bite?"

"Well, no, of course not. It's made of wood."

"Can I feel your beard too?" he asked.

Without considering that a stranger might object to such a request, he moved his head closer to mine and with a squint started to examine the long strands of my untrimmed beard.

And I was again struck by the gentleness emanating from his touch, his whole being.

"Why is it so white?"

"Because I'm old. Old people's beards turn white," I said.

"When I have a beard will it turn white too? My papa's young. His mustache is black." He told me that his father was a "security guard" who goes around a "campus" making sure "everything's all right." That sometimes he rides a bicycle and sometimes a motor scooter. Then he always picks up Giovanni after school and takes him home. And when it isn't raining, he likes to jog along the quayside, while Giovanni waits, swinging his legs on a bench and playing video games on a little device he keeps in his pocket. But this time he had put it back. "Better to play chess with you," he said.

I also learned that besides his papa, Giovanni had a green parakeet named Po-Po with clipped wings, so it couldn't fly. At night, Po-Po would call out, "*Voglio dormire, voglio dormire!*" meaning that it wanted to be put in its cage with a cover over it. And then when it woke up the next morning and wanted to be fed, it would say, "*Mangiare, mangiare!*" Like Po-Po, Giovanni spoke Italian at home. His grandmother, who lives in Perugia, doesn't understand English at all, he informed me. Extending his lips like the bell of a tiny trumpet and rolling the *r*, Giovanni pronounced it *Per-r-r-o-o-ja*. His mama, however, lives far away in Hong Kong. She has a new papa there and a new baby, Giovanni's half-sister, although he's never seen her and misses his mama very much, but his papa said that he won't be able to visit her there just yet-—he needs to be bigger first. Giovanni made a little roof over his head with his hand to show how much bigger he needed to be before he could go to Hong Kong by himself, since his papa would have to work and wouldn't be able to come with him.

We started to play. I was struck by his ability to concentrate, unusual in children his age.

"Should I go easy on you?" he impishly asked after I'd made a few moves.

"No allowances, please," I said and immediately gave away a pawn.

Giovanni looked at me with a serious, studying gaze and then took the pawn. I gave him a knight too. He looked at me again, this time puzzled.

"You can take the move back, if you want," he generously offered. "I'll go easy on you." He had apparently just learned the expression and enjoyed repeating it.

About ten minutes later a solidly built young man with curly hair like Giovanni's and a dark mustache jogged over to us. Even though it was late November, he was wearing only a tank top and shorts. He was Giovanni's father—Giovanni senior. Jogging in place, he said something rapid and severe in Italian. The boy nodded like an adult while nervously squirming,

"Well, we thought we might play a game," I said with a smile, hoping to lighten the atmosphere. "Your son's a great kid! He plays like an grown-up and is about to get the better of me."

Delighted by the praise, which was clearly very important to him, Giovanni jumped down from the bench and started to hop around.

His father took a water bottle from his waistband and tossing his head back, greedily drank.

"You want some? No? Well, that's it, then. We still have grocery shopping to do, and he has to practice his recorder."

Giovanni stopped hopping and his mobile face, which seemed to register the slightest shifts of mood, immediately became sad. He sighed. He didn't want to leave.

"Papa, can we come back tomorrow?" he asked.

"It depends on the weather. If it's raining, there will be no jog," his father said brusquely.

As they were leaving, Giovanni kept looking back at me and waving. And then as they climbed the slope from the quayside to the street above, he either squatted in an amusing way or hopped like a rabbit, meaning to leave me with a final entertaining impression.

4

The next day was sunny, and I went back to the quayside again. There was a piercing west wind, and as I waited, hoping for Giovanni to turn up, I shivered from the wind and the bench's cold steel slats. But he didn't come, and the day, despite its brilliantly glistening blue water and peacefully clinking yachts, lost its charm. But I stayed, watching people pass by and waited. Tumbling over each other, a flock of loudly quacking Mallards emerged from the water and skirting my bench continued up the green slope. The birds weren't at all intimidated by my presence and silently began to forage behind me.

Many birds pass through Vancouver in the fall and early winter on their way south. Some of them remain, and in the fall and winter you can see Wood Ducks, White-winged Scoters, Harlequin ducks, and many other interesting species. Rocking like little painted boats on the water, they occupy a fairly wide expanse of it, and as they move forward in it, they arrange themselves in much the same way they do in group flight. But that day the birds' extravagant plumage gave me no pleasure, as if in Giovanni's absence nature's bounty itself was wasted on me.

Suddenly I got hungry. The idea of having a light meal at Giardino on the Marinaside Crescent, my usual haunt, comforted me for a moment. A section of outdoor tables extends from the restaurant out to the quayside walkway but is separated from it by a low fence of stacked steel tubes. Above the tables is a sort of tinted-glass awning to shield the restaurant's patrons from winter rain and summer sun. Even if it's cold, I usually take a table outside, where the restaurant's relentless music is less audible. The bridge's low rumble can still be heard, but it's somehow just another part of the alien, impersonal landscape. The outdoor tables are mostly empty on the weekdays I go there. Covering my knees with a burgundy comforter provided for that purpose (they're draped over the stainless-steel backs of all the empty chairs), I'm at last able to catch my breath.

On the other side of the fence, not much more than an arm's length away, a woman walks by talking to herself—or so it seems, since she has nothing in her hands. But from her animated tone I realize that she's talking on the phone through a device that I can't see. As if my own fate somehow depended upon it, I strain to capture the tip of her conversation. "By customizing and personalizing the interface ... You'll get loads of options that way ... " Disappointed, I turn away to look at the blue-green mountains and the cloud shadows running along their flank.

A very young waitress (almost a girl) takes my order. Her name is either June or Julia—I can never remember which. She stands with her hands diffidently clasped in front of her starched white apron, and the meticulous care of her appearance is exceptionally pleasing to me: the precise part of her dark, smoothly combed hair, the gleam in her green eyes edged with dark, lightly mascaraed lashes, and especially her little turned-down Peter Pan collar that nobody has worn for decades. Could it be that I have really been taking that route to the dragonfly quayside for the sake of that young woman?

The first time we met, Julia (that really does suit her best) introduced herself to me as an "actor." The word jarred.

A world in which actresses have all turned into "actors" has lost a good deal of its charm to become as bland as oatmeal. And maybe for that reason I didn't ask her where and in what she had performed, silently deciding that she hadn't performed in anything anywhere and that the unhappy word "actor" was really more an expression of her ideal sense of herself, of her Platonic essence, as opposed to her temporary instantiation as a waitress on the dragonfly quay.

But on the day I want to tell about, I was for some reason especially glad to see her.

"A pizza, as usual?"

"Yes. Mushrooms, bell pepper—well, all the regular stuff. And please bring me a small salad too. I'm famished."

"Would you like me to bring the pizza first or the salad?"

"Which one is faster?

"The pizza only needs to be heated."

"Excellent, the pizza, then," I said rubbing my chilled hands together, pleased with the effect my old-fashioned politesse always had on her.

"And a Grandville ale, as usual?"

She remembered, sweet girl! Something was loosened and warmed in me by her response, and it even seemed to me that I was entitled to the ale and to Julia's care and friendly green eyes—as a sort of compensation for Giovanni's absence. After I had finished the pizza and started on the firm, slightly crunchy green leaves of my *verdura mista* salad, I realized that

Chinese white radish—daikon—had been added to it. Whatever for? It was completely out of place and ruined the excellent Italian recipe.

As I was getting ready to pay, Julia suddenly announced that it was her last day. She was moving to London! London?! Had somebody offered her a job there or given her a part? No, there was no part yet, but she had a friend in London, and the friend had a friend, and the friend of her friend said there would be more opportunities there... Opportunities? "Well, certainly there will be more opportunities in London," I muttered, although I wanted to shout, "Wake up! Don't go to any London! You're very pretty, that's true, but you don't know how many pretty little mugs are already knocking on the doors of London theaters. And is Vancouver really so much worse? We have spectacular views, Hollywood shoots ten or more pictures a year here, since it's cheaper. But London—what do you need London for? The grass is always greener on the other side, but in this case the other side is a whole continent and then an ocean!"

I didn't obviously say any of that. What right did I have to meddle in her life? Who was I to her? Nor did I mention that I had a friend there with whom I had studied at University College London. For what help could an old professor of history in London possibly be to a waitress from the Giardino in Vancouver? A waitress, moreover, who wanted to be an "actor"?

We said our farewells and I left her a big tip, but felt even more despondent. My day was irrevocably ruined.

As I was making my way back along the quayside, my legs started to feel heavy and my heart began to pound. But I carried on, anxiously listening to the thumping in my chest. It's something I've experienced for a long time and accompanies fears and anxiety.

In order to calm down and put morbid thoughts out of my mind, I decided to keep walking. Off to the side of the pavement I noticed a construction that I had somehow overlooked before, one whose purpose wasn't clear at all. I took a closer look, walking around it. Inscribed on the four vertical sides of a large Lucite cube was a series of words in which every other one was inverted, so that I had to twist my neck in order to read them: BOX CAR, FLAT CARS, TANK CARS, and in brackets, [TRAM CARS], all of it accompanied by an identifying placard with the unintelligible word string, "The Art master makes a train all built and rebuilt gone and a thousand things leave no trace." Hmm... No trace indeed!

I instinctively turned back toward the restaurant and sat down again on another bench near it. Since it was November and the sun was already beginning to set, I was forced to accept that I wouldn't see my little friend that day. It rained continuously for the next three days after that, and the quayside trek made little sense.

But then it was sunny again and I was hurrying along my usual route. And that time I was lucky. I had barely reached the cube with the railroad gibberish when I saw Giovanni. He was running toward me as fast as he could, radiant with joy.

"Let's play chess until Papa comes back, okay?"

We headed for our old bench, but it was occupied.

"We'll find another," I said, but Giovanni hesitated.

"No, it's better to wait here for a while. Papa said not to leave the dog park."

The "dog park" was Giovanni's name for a small grassy area with large stones placed here and there with a steel sculpture in the center that looks like an asymmetrical jawbone. Dogs were running around the sculpture and stone while heir owners tossed balls to them using red plastic throwers. It was a bright day with a strong breeze. The yachts swayed at their moorings. The hardware attached to their masts clinked in the cold air like crystal goblets.

"What if there's a big wind storm? Then all the ships could sink!" Giovanni said.

"Don't worry, we don't have storms like that here."

"Why not?"

"Well, for one thing, it's a harbor, and for another, we're protected by mountains. See!"

I took him in my hands and carefully, so I wouldn't lose my balance, lifted him up so he could get a better look at the mountains. It was the first time his eyes were at the same level as mine. But instead of looking at the mountains, he carefully examined my face, and especially my beard touching it again with his small gentle fingers.

"You see, mountains all around. On the right and the left, each one higher than the one in front of it, as far as you can see. And that one over there looks like a sleeping auntie with her arms folded across her breast..."

"What's the auntie-mountain's name?" Giovanni asked, putting his arm around my neck and finally turning to look.

"It's called Grouse Mountain, after a kind of bird."

"If Grouse Mountain wasn't there, could there be a big wind storm?

"Perhaps."

"And all the ships could sink?"

"What makes you think that? If they took the ships farther out to sea, they wouldn't sink. The most dangerous storm waves are near the shore, but out in the ocean it isn't so bad."

The expression on his face suddenly changed and his little eyebrows twitched. He was thinking about something else.

"Then I'll go on a big ship to visit my mama in Hong Kong. I'll go by myself with Po-Po."

"But Hong Kong's very, very far away! It would be much easier to go on an airplane!"

"But if I go on a ship, I might see a big fish."

"You mean a whale?"

"No, a very big fish," Giovanni mysteriously replied.

Suddenly he stuck his nose in my beard, awkwardly making a kissing sound and started to laugh at his prank. Enveloped by a milky smell, I realized that his chin was smeared with something. I put him down and reached in my pocket for my handkerchief.

"Were you eating something?"

"There was ice cream at school. They only had vanilla. My favorite is chocolate."

"Do you like school?

Giovanni nodded.

"What do you like best about it?

"I like drawing and music. I like everything the best."

"And the teachers?"

"I like Miss MacGregor and Miss Sherwood and Miss Giompuolis. I like all the teachers the best."

"I used to be a teacher too. I taught philosophy." For some reason, I wanted to test him, to surprise him with an unfamiliar word.

"When I grow up, I'll also ... also ... I'll also ... teach *philostrophy*!" he immediately assured me, clearly wanting to say something that would please me.

"Do your know what it is?"

"Yup!" He paused for a second and then impishly replied, "I knew yesterday."

"Let me see if I can explain it. Well, one way to think about it is that philosophy teaches us how to be good, so we'll be happy. How to think and do the right things ... You see?"

"Are you good?" Giovanni asked.

The question caught me by surprise.

"Well ... I'm not sure. Probably, not very. Probably, I'm good sometimes and sometimes I'm not, depending on the circumstances. But I always try to be good."

"Santa Clause is always good."

"Do you really think I'm Santa Claus?"

Giovanni smiled and silently nodded.

"So that's it! That must mean that I didn't really know who I was until I met you. Maybe I am Santa Claus, after all!"

"Why didn't you know who you are?" Giovanni asked, obviously confused by the idea.

"Do you know who you are?"

"I am me!" Giovanni exclaimed and he spread his arms wide like an adult. He was amazed that such a simple truth wasn't obvious to me.

"That's certainly true! You, little friend, couldn't possibly be mixed up with anybody else. But with other things it isn't always so easy. Sometimes it's clear what a thing is and sometimes it isn't. Take chess, for example. There are chess pieces, right? And there are the game's rules. But is it so clear that neither could exist without the other? On the one hand, they could exist, but on the other maybe they couldn't. And which came first, the chess pieces or the rules, is hard to say."

Why on earth was I trying to explain such a conundrum to a young child? But it was too late. Giovanni stared at me dumbstruck, or rather at the opening in my beard from which flew sounds that had no meaning for him.

I got out my little chess set, opened it, and picked up a knight.

"You see this knight? It's small. But at home you have

a bigger chess set, and the knights are bigger too. Maybe they even look different. And they're made of wood instead of plastic like this one. Chess sets can look different, but we can still play with them if we know the rules. With big sets and little ones and wooden ones and plastic ones, right?"

"Yes," Giovanni said, continuing with unwavering attention to study my mouth. He was waiting, trying to understand what I was getting at.

"And if we took away the board and hid all the pieces and decided to play the game in our heads, with an invisible set, would that be something we could do?"

Giovanni skeptically tipped his head to the side with a slight frown.

"Why not, then?"

"Because I never tried it. I never tried to play invisibly."

I laughed and gave him a quick hug. The precocious quickness, insight, and receptivity of his mind had endeared him to me. I started to think that in his own way he could probably understand Plato's cave parable as well as some of my eighteen-year-olds had. And it even seemed to me that I might be able to hint to him in some way that I was often overwhelmed by a feeling of the unreality, the insubstantiality of the world, a feeling that had grown more pronounced after Priss died.

Teaching Plato for many years and talking about the world of Forms, which despite its inaccessibility and invisibility was the only true world, and talking about the reflection of that Platonic world in our material, physical one, I would, in my efforts to convince the students of the grandeur of Plato's conception, passionately defend his position as if it were my own. Did I in fact believe in an ideal world of Forms beyond this one? For me, that world existed as a reality that I would be able to grasp only if I could summon the spiritual strength, the spiritual daring to do so. But the longer I've lived, and the weaker my powers have become, the more inaccessible that ideal has seemed. But that day with Giovanni it suddenly struck me that I had at last found the until then elusive point of contact between the blessedly heavenly and the merely earthly.

It was, trite though it will sound, concentrated in the palm of Giovanni's hand that lay in my own, and in the searching gaze of his dark, wide-spaced eyes. He too had apparently sensed something, and taking hold of my jacket, he became still, pressing his curly little head against my chest. My throat tightened, I couldn't speak, and I just lightly smoothed his dark curls. Then he let go of my hand and said,

"Okay, now it's my turn to ask a riddle. It's, it's hmm ... " And he suddenly broke free of me, jumped down, and ran after a large Glaucous gull. The startled bird immediately took flight, flashing the snow-white underside of its wings. He followed it with his eyes.

"I know! Guess this! Why ... Why, hmm, why do

birds have two wings?"

I thought about it for a moment. How should I answer? Because they couldn't fly with just one? Wouldn't be able to keep themselves aloft? I thought that such a thing would already have been obvious to perceptive little Giovanni and that he must have had something else in mind. And trying to explain the nature of bird flight would have been much too complicated anyway.

"I give up," I said.

"You give up?! You do?!" he said, spinning in happy excitement like a top. "But I know! I know why! Because only one wing would be ugly!"

It turned out that he placed symmetry, balance, the equipoise of the world, at the apex of his triangle, seeing in it the first cause and indispensable condition of all the world's arrangements.

But what if the symmetry of double wings only seems beautiful to us because it satisfies the laws of physics?

"You didn't guess, so it's my turn again!" Giovanni exclaimed, taking my silence for agreement and pleased with what he regarded as his obvious superiority. "Can you guess what my favorite number is?"

"Well, that certainly is a hard question. . . Even harder than the first. Probably something large! A hundred, or a thousand, or a million?"

"You didn't guess! You didn't!" Giovanni kept jumping up and down. "My favorite number is six!"

"Six? So little?" I said, and made an astonished face.

"Tomorrow I'll be six! That's why!" He held up one hand with its five fingers splayed and the other hand with its index finger extended. "That many!"

"Well, then you really are a big boy! Happy birthday!"

"And will you come to my birthday party tomorrow? Please come! Please!" Giovanni tipped his head to the side and made a miserable face.

"I'd be glad to, only we'll have to ask your papa first," I said hesitatingly.

"He won't mind! He won't mind! Samantha and Peter and Douglas will be there. Douglas is my best friend. There he is, there's Papa!"

Farther down the knoll near the water's edge a crowd had gathered to look at something on the ground. Giovanni pulled me after him. His father was standing with his back to us, bent over with his hands on his knees. In the center of the crowd knelt a man of about forty with an impassive face. In his hands was a black box with buttons, but his attention was fixed instead on what looked like a large mechanical spider. It quietly hummed and flashed tiny lights, stuck out four steel legs, and then, gently swaying, began to rise straight up in the air. It described two wide circles over the marina, and then, responding to the console in it's owner's hands, it retuned to its original spot. Giovanni watched transfixed as it retracted its legs, turned off its lights, and was still.

"How much did that thing cost?" Giovanni senior

asked the machine's impassive owner.

The latter mumbled something in reply without taking his eyes off his toy.

And then he tucked it under his arm and quickly set off along the quayside in the direction of Burrard Bridge. The crowd dispersed.

Giovanni senior wiped invisible sweat from his brow with the back of his hand and shook his head.

"Two thousand grand! Some toy!" he said. And then he added, "I see that you've become buddies with my son."

"Yes, we've been asking each other riddles. Giovanni asked why a bird has two wings. I wanted to say that otherwise it couldn't fly, but now I see that I was wrong. That thing could fly very well without any wings at all."

"Papa, can we buy one too?"

"What do you think?"

"That we won't," Giovanni sighed. "Papa, can I invite this Santa Clause to my birthday party?" Giovanni senior gave me the once-over of a professional policeman.

"Santa Clause? Hmm, I thought Santa Clause only comes on Christmas. It's still the end of November, I believe. And wouldn't it be pretty boring for your Santa Claus friend with all your little guys?"

"Please, Papa, please," Giovanni pleaded, twisting his comical little mug.

"You see what a sociable little fellow I have. He starts up friendships right on the street. By the way, would you mind staying with him another ten or fifteen minutes, so I can do another run? Down to the bridge and back? Well, I actually have no objection to the birthday party, if you really want to come," Giovanni senior said.

I said that he could jog as long as he liked, that Giovanni and I had been having a good time, and that there was nothing for him to worry about.

The birthday party was to take place the next day, Saturday, at noon. Vaguely gesturing toward the high-rises beyond the knoll, Giovanni-Senior named their address and trotted away.

"Let's walk around a little and then play chess," I said to Giovanni.

Giovanni pulled me away from the direction his father had gone.

"What kind of present are you going to give me?" he asked.

"I don't know. I'll have to think about it."

5

I gazed at the marina and yachts and boats, and remembered the splendid model of the Swedish galleon *Vasa* that I had bought many years before on a visit to Stockholm. Made of different kinds of wood, the model replicated with masterful precision all the details of the famous seventeenth-century warship that had capsized just as it was leaving Stockholm harbor on its maiden voyage. I imagined the interest Giovanni's little fingers would take in the decorations of its high flat stern, the intricate carving of its bowsprit, its square-rigged sails ... I imagined how I would linger on some pretext, and then, after the Samanthas and Peters and Douglases had left, how Giovanni and I would sit down on a sofa somewhere in a corner and I would tell him everything I knew about the ship: what a beautiful vessel it had been; how in order to amaze the world the builders had added an additional deck of bronze cannons, which very likely made the ship so top-heavy that it keeled over and sank from the first strong breeze even before it had reached the open sea. I would tell him how three hundred years later, at a great risk to themselves, divers had helped to bring it up from the bottom after removing the remaining cannons and freeing the ship from the mud into which it had sunk.

"Well, have you thought of anything?" Giovanni asked, deciding that he'd given me enough time.

"But if I tell you now, it won't be a surprise."

"Well, give me just a hint. Please!"

"A hint? Well, all right. My present's something that floats."

"A seagull?"

"No, you haven't guessed."

"A boat?"

"You've getting warm ... Warm ... Okay, I'll tell you. Not a boat but a ship."

"A real one?"

"No, a model, only it's so perfect that it's just like a real one."

Giovanni was silent, the ends of his little mouth drooping. I could see that he was disappointed.

"Don't worry, it's a very beautiful model. You've never seen anything like it. You can look at it from every angle and inside and out, something you can't do with a real ship."

But he still didn't say anything. And then his lips suddenly started to tremble with his bottom lip creeping up over his upper one. He was about to start crying. My heart skipped a beat.

"What is it? What's the matter, sweetheart?"

"I don't need a ship because...because I lost my recorder."

He couldn't help himself and started to sob inconsolably.

At first I didn't understand what he meant, but then from his disjointed account I was able to piece together the catastrophe that had befallen my little friend in the four days since I had seen him. He and his father had gone to Ikea to buy a little table on rollers, and first they went to the different floors together and his papa picked out what he wanted, but when they got back downstairs, he remembered that they needed some bathroom hooks too, and he left Giovanni in the play area while he went to look for them. Giovanni started to play with another little boy there and got a Transformer out of his backpack to show him, and his recorder was in the backpack too, since they had gone to Ikea right after his music lesson, and maybe he didn't put the recorder back in the backpack after he got the Transformer out, or maybe he did put it back, but when they got home it wasn't there anymore.

His papa still didn't know about it, but when he found out, he would yell at him, since the recorder was expensive and his papa was very strict.

I drew the little boy towards me and smoothed his hair.

"I'll buy you a new one. Don't cry, little friend, don't cry, kiddo."

"But Papa will ask where it is, and I...don't know."

"I'll talk to your papa. Everything will be all right, I promise."

He pressed against me, quietly whimpering. It broke my heart to see my happy, sunny little Giovanni crying.

I got home in a mild panic, but there was still enough time. I drank a quick cup of coffee and, barely catching my breath, drove to a music store. The clerk showed me a shiny black soprano recorder for $35 that he thought would be appropriate for a six-year-old. I of course had no idea what kind of recorder Giovanni had lost, but it didn't matter. I had no doubt that I'd be able to smooth things with his father, whatever kind it had been. The ship model was in a special glass case in my study. That morning it would never have occurred to me to part with it, but now everything had changed. I decided to give Giovanni both the model and the recorder. I

couldn't find a suitable box for the model, which was almost a
meter long and bulky even with its masts and sails removed, so
I emptied three smaller boxes and used their cardboard to make
another box of the necessary size, which kept me busy for
quite a while. Tired, but with a feeling of having accomplished
something worthwhile, I finally went to bed.

The next morning I got up early. After breakfast, I took
a shower, trimmed my beard, evened out the shaggy bristles of
my eyebrows, and put on my best three-piece suit and a bowtie.
I grinned at my reflection in the mirror. When was the last
time I had worn a bowtie? Just after Priss died, probably. The
Seattle Opera had brought *Parsifal* to town and I got tickets to
celebrate Brigid's sixty-fifth birthday.

I splashed on some cologne, put on my black, rather
old-fashioned but still excellent cashmere overcoat, and
cradling the model in its large box in my arms went out to the
garage. Then realizing that I'd forgotten the recorder, I ran to
get it after putting the box in the back seat.

I looked for a parking space near the quayside a long
time, and then when I did fine one and had put ten dollars
in the meter, I saw that I'd made a mistake. It was in an area
where the spaces were reserved for the exclusive use of the
nearby yacht club. As, presumably, the large Chinese characters
on the sign had announced, with the information I had failed
to notice written in English in little letters below. I circled
around another twenty minutes or so under the bridge, under
its branching off-ramps and crossings, afraid I would be late.

Finally in desperation, I placed the *Handicapped* sign left
from Priss on the dashboard and parked in the first space of
that kind I came to.

   I put the recorder in my overcoat pocket and got the
big box with the model out of the back seat. As I was trying
to manage all that, I suddenly started sweating, even though
it was cold. And then with the box at last cradled in my arms
and the recorder sticking out of my pocket, I started to climb
the knoll toward the high-rises where my little friend lived,
even though I didn't know his address but had written it down
on a piece of paper. I put the box down on the grass and went
through all the pockets of my coat, my jacket, my vest, my
pants, but still couldn't find it. I started to sweat again. Where
had I left it? In the hallway? On my desk? In the kitchen?
Should I go back and look for it? If I missed his birthday
party, Giovanni might think I had let him down, but there was
nothing else I could do.

   Picking up the box, I hurried back to the car. But after
I had already driven halfway back over the bridge, I suddenly
remembered that there had never been a piece of paper with
the address, since Giovanni senior had simply called out the
street and number as he was leaving. And that something
about the address had struck me at the time, but what? Oh,
yes! the street name! *Homer*! For there is in our city a street
that runs through the center from north to south and was
very likely named for the owner of a mine or a sawmill, like
everything else in Vancouver.

But I preferred not to think about mines or sawmills then. My Giovanni could only have lived on a street named after the real Homer who wrote that Poseidon *still raged and seethed against the great Odysseus until he reached his native shore.*

As soon as I crossed the bridge, I turned around again and drove back to the quayside. This time I was able to find a parking place at once. I almost ran to the high-rises. There they were, an indistinguishable cluster of dragonfly dwellings. And hidden in them was the one human soul I needed! But how would I be able to tell which of those buildings was his? And even if I did somehow recognize the building number, how would I identify the apartment, since I didn't even know his last name? Obviously, the situation was hopeless.

After I got back to the car a second time, sweating even more profusely and completely exhausted, a light rain started to fall. I put the gifts back in the car and tried not to despair, comforting myself with the thought that I could go to the quayside the next day and explain to Giovanni what had happened and that everything would be the same as it had been before. I even left the gifts in the back seat when I got home, so sure was I that I would see him the next day.

Once home I was overcome with such enormous fatigue that I couldn't even brush my teeth or pull back the covers on my bed. Without undressing, I lay down in the darkness, listening to the loud, irregular thumping of my heart. For no reason, I was in a cold sweat again and overcome with

unbearable anxiety. I clenched my teeth to keep from being
completely overwhelmed by it, but then an agonizing pain
suddenly gripped my jaw and quickly spread to my neck and
shoulder. When it let go, I couldn't catch my breath.

I don't remember calling an ambulance or being taken
to the hospital. From the long weeks of recovery I remember
only the broad face of Brigid, hovering over me and again
moving away.

It wasn't until the beginning of March that I was able to
go to quayside again. The sharp light reflected from the white
concrete and stainless-steel hurt my eyes as before. A motley,
busy crowd moved along the quayside in a continuous stream.
Everything around me seemed to be running or flying, with the
bicycle riders hurtling toward me like a moving wall.

But I never saw Giovanni again.

Later on I did encounter him in a dream. The first
time he was standing on the bow of a magnificent old galleon
with a parrot on his shoulder. I understood that he was on his
way to visit his mother in Hong Kong. But the second time
we were sailing together and I felt with my whole broken,
damaged heart, that we would never part again, that we
were one. He had returned to me from the depths of my own
childhood, a shy little boy with dark, curly hair and a recorder,
and I was Giovanni and he was me. And my mother, and
Priscilla, and everyone, all the other people in my long life,
were alive, and loved by me the way they had not been in the
past, and the lapping of a matte-white wave merged with the

gentle modulations of the innocent, childlike music Giovanni and I made together.

Returning

1

I had enough money for about three months and no more. I remember being overcome with a strange apathy and instead of taking some action, sitting till evening on deserted Jericho Beach, counting the barges on English Bay and gazing at the still unfamiliar mountain landscape across the water in front of me.

As the sun set behind Vancouver Island on my left, the peaks to the north and northwest turned into stark silhouettes against the rapidly fading sky, with torn patches of fog starting to creep down the nearer slopes toward the dimming water. The prisms of the skyscrapers across the bay began to light up from within like luminescent deep-dwelling fish, and the mountains and water seemed to merge and then dissolve in the darkness until it was impossible to make out much of anything except the lights of the pulsing human anthill on the opposite shore and those of the barges, their glimmering reflections in the motionless water suggesting a beautiful, enticingly magical life within.

I had joined my boyfriend, Carlos Perreira, in Vancouver after he was offered the position of resident choreographer with Ballet BC. I have to admit, however, that it was more than a wish to follow him that led me to abandon the life I had made for myself in Montréal. My wanderlust has always looked for a pretext.

Every transposition in space tears from the temporal
continuum a stretch of no-man's land. The discarded past
temporarily loses its hold, while the future remains to be
discovered like some living and breathing land beyond the
horizon's mysterious haze.

What inspired thoughts, what bold, adventurous plans
swarm in your head as you sit on
your suitcase! How fresh life feels, how equally possible
everything seems as you wait at the crossroads with no step yet
taken in any direction!

It was with good reason that Carlos had called me a
"tumbleweed" and said that there could be no making a home
with me, since because of my weight—forty-two kilos, the
same as my age at the time—gravity had no affect on me.
The slight proved a source of particular grief when I learned
that the position of répétiteur at Ballet BC that I thought had
been promised to me had been given instead to a cousin of
the company's artistic director, leaving me without work in a
strange city. Looking back on it now, I can see that my own
recklessness had played a mean trick on me that time too. The
promise had actually been quite vague with nothing in writing.
But as I've always done, I decided to risk it anyway, putting
my hopes in Carlos' connections.

The mutual reproaches had already begun to sway the
already wobbly little tent of our union, and then Carlos' affair
with a young girl in the corps de ballet brought it to an end
and the tent collapsed. Six months after arriving in Vancouver,

Carlos and I split up. Although I didn't say so at the time, I was glad to receive as my share this glass and stainless-steel city nestled in the middle of such rare natural beauty.

In the studio apartment I rented on the top floor of an ugly prefabricated building after our breakup, in summer it was possible to breathe only after dark. The venetian blind with its cheap plastic slats reached only partway down the window, and by afternoon the room was unbearably hot. The building opposite had just had a new roof installed, and the blinding rays reflected from its corrugated steel filled the room from early morning with an oppressive gleam. Since retiring from professional performance at the age of thirty-six, I had continued to do ballet exercises every morning, just as before. But for those *pliés, tendus battements*, and *jetés* in my new lodging I had to cover my eyes with a scarf as in blind man's bluff.

After an early breakfast (a cup of black coffee and half a banana) I would visit the free tennis courts in Stanley Park and for about forty minutes hit a ball against a wall. Since I still didn't know anyone in the city, there was nobody to partner with. After tennis, I would walk around the city. How different it was from the Montréal I had left behind!

In Montréal I had taught in a ballet academy while also trying my hand at ballet and theatre reviewing. Apparently, I had some ability, or maybe I was simply lucky, or maybe Montréal was just favorable soil for my new profession. Whatever the case, I had some success. People started paying attention to my opinions, and a negative review from me could even affect the box office. I thus had a certain notoriety in performing circles. Even though the Montréal economy was in recession, the city was of course still one of the country's main music and theatre centers. The best-known European ballet companies came to visit, and since Boston and New York weren't very far away, it wasn't especially hard to go to either for a show and then write a review of it.

Deprived of connections and sources of income in unfamiliar Vancouver, I really needed to take some action quickly. But instead I sat on the beach for days, gazing at the barges and mountains. And then on one of those anxious, confused days Carlos' sister, Stella, called me from Montréal. She and I had become friends and she knew about the breakup and want to help. Through her Chilean husband she was acquainted with the entire Chilean community on both sides of the continent. One of her husband's friends in Vancouver, a "real gentleman," as she put it, was looking for people to contribute to a new magazine. "He used to be a big cheese in the Chilean government and now he's decided to publish a magazine. He needs something about cinema. Call him and see."

And that's how I met Laureano Santalone.

2

The doorman of a tall building on Alberni Street let me into the lobby, which was decorated with the obligatory pot of artificial orchids on a stand and dark-blue marble panels separated by mirrors reflecting tall Chinese vases in all the corners.

Compared to my own unsettled circumstances at the time, Santalone's apartment seemed as I entered it to be the epitome of bourgeois comfort. Heavy velvet drapes darkened my host's study and the reflected glow of a fireplace played on the gilded bindings of a wide bookcase. Laureano looked to be about sixty-five. His aristocratic bearing, refined manners, and old-fashioned courtesy were from a now almost vanished world. His elegantly lean figure and tall stature, the impeccable cut of his dark suit, fine features of his elongated face and pointed beard—he had as if stepped out of a classic Spanish portrait. I later learned from the long conversations we had that Castilian blood did in fact flow in his veins. His ancestors had come to the New World from Spain in the eighteenth century.

Laureano was reserved in manner yet simple and cordial. Gracious hospitality and solicitude are common features of good breeding, but it seemed to me then that those agreeable qualities existed exclusively for me. But who has not taken something desired as real? There's no doubt, however, that Laureano was a man of rare charm. I'm sure I wasn't the only one who felt more intelligent, kinder, and better in his presence.

On that first visit, my host placed before me a silver tray with two crystal goblets. As I was sipping the mixed drink he made for us, a woman in a clumsily cut short skirt stretched over fat thighs looked in on us. Strings of red coral beads lay upon on her powerful bosom. "What a vulgar maid he has!"

I involuntarily thought. The woman gave my slight figure a once-over, and then said something rapidly and vehemently to Laureano in Spanish. "Let me introduce my wife, Rosalia," he said. I got up to shake her hand but failed to do so since she had already left.

We began to talk about Laureano's new magazine. The idea was that it would be primarily for the city's Latin American diaspora and would be in both English and Spanish. "I don't know Spanish," I pointed out. "It doesn't matter. Write in English and I'll translate it. So far you and I are the only ones on the staff," he said with a smile.

Laureano intended to write a political overview for the first issue and offered "culture" to me. It was 1998 and the centenary of Eisenstein's birth, and he wanted an article about the unfinished documentary *¡Que viva Mexico!*

As it turned out, a great deal in Laureano's life was tied to Mexico. He had after the fall of Allende in 1973 spent the first ten years of his exile in Mexico and had met his wife there. Although I'd never written anything about film, confining myself in Montréal to theatre and ballet productions, as I mentioned, Laureano's idea appealed to me. Eisenstein had interested me ever since I was a young dancer with the Omsk State Music Theatre in Siberia. The theatre's artistic director was from Kazakhstan, from Almaty, where he had met the supervisor of the magnificent dances in the second part of Eisenstein's *Ivan the Terrible,* and his stories about it are something I'll always remember. When Laureano heard that, he became quite animated.

"Wonderful! Wonderful!' he said, splaying his pale, slender fingers like two fans to make a pyramid with their tips—a habit, as I would learn. "You see what kind of coincidences there are! Well, you already have the cards in your hand and will very likely be interested in the other things I can provide. As you certainly know, two Communist artists, David Siqueiros and Diego Rivera, acquainted Eisenstein with Mexico, and they accompanied him on his travels around the country in 1931. I myself knew Siqueiros. I even have two letters from him."

"You knew Siqueiros?! The same Siqueiros who took part in the first attempt on Trotsky's life?" I said, making no attempt to temper my astonishment.

"Yes, the same one. I myself painted in my youth and like other young left-leaning artists, I had been impressed by Siqueiros's famous Barcelona Manifesto for a new revolutionary form of art. I met him two years before he died. He was already an old man then and had aged a lot during his time in prison, but he remained unbroken. I don't know which one was greater in him: his artistic or his revolutionary passion."

Laureano fell silent for a moment.

"Siqueiros was a man of radical views, you know, and a confirmed Stalinist. His Stalinist sympathies were not, it goes without saying, something I shared."

He picked up his pipe and with a quick look at me said,

"Do you mind if I smoke? I can go out onto the balcony. My wife always chases me out there, so I'm used to it."

"Oh no, it won't bother me," I lied, startled at the same time by how easily I did.

Laureano started filling his pipe.

"I didn't know Siqueiros was arrested after the attempt on Trotsky. I thought Stalin had helped him to escape to Moscow."

"Well, it's unlikely that Stalin rescued anybody from persecution," Laureano said as he waved a cloud of smoke away from me. "Even if Siqueiros's connections with Moscow and the NKVD were very strong. No, after the attempt on Trotsky he didn't suffer any harm. He was given a plane ticket and expelled from Mexico and ultimately made his way to us in Chile. You of course know who Pablo Neruda is, our famous Chilean poet. He was the Chilean ambassador to Mexico at the time and helped Siqueiros with the move to Chile. At first, the Chilean government wouldn't allow Siqueiros in the capital. His radical views were too dangerous. So he and his family settled in Chillán. It's unlikely you've ever heard of it—a little provincial town. But it's famous now, thanks to Siqueiros's *Muerte al Invasor*, the enormous mural he painted on the walls and ceiling of the local school library."

"So you knew him in the 1940s?"

"Oh my goodness, no! I was still a child then. I met him in 1972. As one of my bureaucratic responsibilities, it fell to me to arrange a celebration that year for the thirtieth anniversary of *Muerte al Invasor*. I organized festivities in Chillán, and Siqueiros came to Chile for them. He was touched by the attention he received and wrote me two letters and gave me a copy of another one he had received from Eisenstein himself. I don't know, maybe you could find a way to use it in your article? I'll leave that up to you. May I refill your glass?"

"No, thanks... When would you like the article?" I asked, more and more intrigued by the unusual person to whom fate had led me.

"There's no hurry. The magazine's only in the organizational stage, with the financial question still unresolved."

Despite that slightly alarming news about funding, my conversation with Laureano had inspired me and I enthusiastically got to work on the article.

The story of *¡Que viva Mexico!* is one of the more tragic in Eisenstein's biography. Already a world-famous director thanks to *Battleship Potemkin* and *October*, he had been sent by Stalin to Hollywood in 1930 to study the new technique of talking cinema. After cordial meetings there (Douglas Fairbanks and Mary Pickford entertained him at their Beverly Hills mansion) and a contract for financing with the famous progressive writer Upton Sinclair and his wife, Eisenstein and his cameraman Eduard Tisse and assistant director Grigory Alexandrov set off for Mexico to realize their dream of making a documentary about the country and

Returning

its recent revolution. The filming, however, encountered difficulties. Eisenstein was unable to keep either to the budget or the deadline indicated in his contract with the Sinclairs' production company, and in the end Stalin ordered him to return home. He had in the meantime sent well over 50,000 meters of exposed film to Hollywood for processing, the last he would ever see of it, despite attempts to sent it to him. That separation from the fruits of his labor he viewed as a personal catastrophe, one that he was unable to get over for many years. It was only in 1979, thirty-one years after his death, that a version edited by Alexandrov was finally shown—a pale shadow of the grand plan Eisenstein seems to have had in mind.

Laureano was pleased with the finished article but couldn't pay for it. Since the magazine's sponsors were, he said, still delaying its funding, the business was stalled, and our collaboration therefore came to an end. When I realized I would no longer have any reason to see him, I was gripped by a sort of panic.

I knew he gave private lessons in Spanish in his home. Might he take me on as a student? To my amazement he agreed, although he wouldn't accept any money.

"I am in your debt. Permit me in this way to express my gratitude to you," he said with a gentle and with what seemed to me a sad smile.

Since I knew some French and had picked up a bit of Spanish from Carlos, I had a sort of working knowledge of colloquial Spanish and thought I might even be able to start speaking it in a few months. But to take advantage of Laureano's services that long without payment wasn't something I couldn't bring myself to do. We wrangled a long time over our mutual generosity, assuring each other that for both of us "the ideals of art and culture were higher than any material considerations." In the end, we agreed to trade languages. Laureano would teach me Spanish and I would practice English with him: although he could read and understand English well, he felt he needed to be able to speak it with greater colloquial fluency. So we conversed this way: I spoke to him in English and he answered me in Spanish, and then we switched roles, with the English tending to predominate on both sides whenever the subject took over, as it often did.

What did we talk about? Laureano had arrived in Vancouver the year before I did, and so naturally we compared our impressions of the city. Could a refined aesthete raised in the tradition of "European culture," despite his own deep New World origins, really like a young, Americanized metropolis on the Pacific coast of Canada? Or was he praising Vancouver out of politeness, having set himself the rule of criticizing neither the cities into which fate deposited him, nor any of their inhabitants either? By training he was a historian and jurist, but not a single university in Vancouver took any interest in him. Left with nothing to do, he had come up with the idea of a magazine. I noticed that any reference to it got from Rosalia only a skeptical smirk. She seemed to regard her husband's ventures with disdain and to view the magazine as just another of his pipedream. Laureano, on the other hand, always spoke of her with warmth and respect.

I saw Rosalia only occasionally, but each time I was struck by something coarse in her face and mode of dress that stood in stark contrast to Laureano's aristocratic elegance. He was unhurriedly courteous, while his wife was hasty, brusque, and peremptory. What connected those two people was a mystery to me. For her part, Rosalia was suspicious of me too. She did in any case convey with every one of her gestures that she had no time to stand on ceremony or waste it in chitchat.

As it turned out, Rosalia Merandelos occupied the important post of cultural affairs officer in the Mexican consulate in Vancouver, although I've never met anyone who less resembled her profession than she did. She must, however, be given her due. She knew languages, was evidently a good administrator, and probably had other qualities that ensured her success in the Mexican diplomatic service. Before Canada, she had been the cultural affairs officer in several other consulates, including in Argentina, Spain, and the United States.

As the unemployed husband of a diplomat wife who was very likely fifteen years younger than he was, Laureano had followed her from country to country.

3

During one of our weekly sessions Laureano and I were talking about dreams. It seemed odd to me that a person as sophisticated and erudite as Laureano would ascribe any meaning at all to them. I remembered my own only rarely, and if I could reproduce them, it would only be in dance.

"Last night I had a dream about my son," Laureano said. "He was around the same age he is in this portrait."

Laureano took from the bookcase a small pencil sketch in a wooden frame. Don Quixote with Laureano's face, a pot on his head, and wearing a breastplate and pantaloons fastened at the knee stood with his thick caricatured legs spread wide apart. In his extended left hand he held a book. Squinting through spectacles about to slide off his thin hooked nose, the Knight of Doleful Countenance was struggling to make out what the book contained. In his right hand were the halter of a skinny nag with a little guy of about ten astride it. The boy's narrow face and sharp chin were just like his father's, and he stared from the picture with wide-set eyes without smiling. Perched on his curly head was a black kitten with its back arched. The drawing's grace and economy of line were those of an exceptional artist.

"My son, Emilio," Laureano said. "It really does looks like him. The artist was a friend of mine and a talented caricaturist, and he gave me the portrait when I visited him in prison to say goodbye before I left Chile. My son was never without cats, and Gilberto depicted him with his favorite, Patroclus. But to return to our subject. We were talking about dreams. Last night I dreamed that my son and I were climbing a high mountain trail in search of an enchanted spring. I had read to him as a boy an Aztec legend about such a place. Whoever stepped into the waters of the mysterious spring would regain whatever he had lost. My son understood it in his own way: if he lost something, a toy soldier, say, the enchanted stream would return it to him. But the legend, obviously, was about people dear to us. So I dreamed that we were climbing higher and higher, and the trees gave way to stunted bushes, and then the bushes disappeared and we entered a region of alpine meadows. Emilio would break away and scamper forward, and then once again I would feel the warmth of his hand in mine. And then there were no meadows anymore, only rocks and the roar of cataracts. Finally, deep in a stone basin, we came upon a spring. The water in the basin seemed as still and smooth as oil. I felt a sudden flood of happiness, for we had found not only the river of return but its very source! And then Emilio shook off his sandals and a moment later would have leapt into the pool! It was only at the last instant that I was able to grab him by his shirt ... "

Laureano lapsed into thought.

"I was overcome with horror, and then I woke up, as usually happens."

"But why horror? Wasn't the spring enchanted?"

"Well, according to the legend, whoever stepped in the river of return would become blind. Only that way could he be joined with those he cared about. A sighted person wouldn't be able to hold an image in his memory with the same fullness and vividness that a blind person could. My son was too young, and I had kept the explanation of the legend from him. A moment later in the dream and I wouldn't have been able to stop him. Nevertheless, when I woke up, it was with joy. For the dream had given me the gift of the living presence of my son, the very thing that reality could not give me. I saw Emilio as clearly as I see you now. The sun gilded his dark chestnut curls and I felt the warmth of his hair with my hand ... "

Evidently overwhelmed with emotion, Laureano fell silent again, and then softly asked,

"Would you like a cookie or perhaps some chocolate?"

"No, no, thank you, don't trouble yourself."

"Ah, yes, I forgot. You don't eat that sort of thing," Laureano grinned as he stepped over to the shelf and put the portrait back.

"If you don't mind my asking, does your son live in Chile now?"

"Yes, of course, of course ... He's grown up now. But the last time I saw him he was the age he is in the portrait."

4

During one of our sessions, at the very end, Laureano said that he would have to cancel the next one, since he and his wife had a reception planned the same day. I hoped that meant that he wasn't going to cancel the lesson entirely but would reschedule it for a another day the same week, but he didn't. "How am I going to manage without him for two whole weeks? No, that's crazy! Am I a child?" I rebuked myself as I rode the elevator back down to the lobby. The doorman and I exchanged our usual nods as I left. I didn't feel like going back to my empty apartment, so I went to English Bay Beach instead.

A scavenger was waving the wand of a metal detector over its damp sand. Fog had obscured the mountains to the north, merging the water with the milky whiteness of the sky. A listless wave slapped against a log, first rolling it toward the shore, then drawing it back out into the bay. Logs of the same kind were spread in parallel rows along the whole length of the beach, where they served as benches. I saw down on one. A large Glaucous gull fearlessly alighted on the other end, its yellow bill with a reddish spot at the tip and black rings around its yellow corneas plainly visible. A light drizzle had begun to fall. I thought with lucid distress about the succession of monotonous days filled with nothing of interest, a gap in time the length of two weeks. I began to shiver as if the temperature had suddenly fallen. The solitary log continued to beat against the sand, trying to move back up onto dry ground like a living thing. Suddenly something struck me from within. My loneliness was replaced by a feeling of fullness and I was no longer aware of the cold. Laureano was standing next to me, very close, by my shoulder, and like me mutely gazing at the smooth grey surface of the water. I grew calmer. "Look how the waves are burnishing the log," I said without turning around, lest I scare the vision away: "See, it has reddish-orange insides like candy filling. It's a Western Red Cedar."

"There aren't any in Chile," I answered for Laureano.

It started raining harder. My hands were turning blue from the cold.

"Let's get under the trees," I suggested.

"Which do you like better, the woods or the sea?" Laureano asked.

"The woods. The sea seems lifeless to me. An enormous watery desert. But we're lucky. We have both woods and the sea, and mountains too, all within reach. You're getting wet. Come over here under my umbrella." I imagined taking him by the arm and to conceal my excitement starting to speak rapidly. "Not far from here, by the entrance to Stanley Park, just before you get to the tennis courts, there's a colony of nesting Great Blue Herons. You want to see it?"

I got up from the log and set off for Stanley Park, still imagining that Laureano was with me. "See, up there high in the trees, they're repairing their nests. An entire colony of them... The nests look like huge worn-out fur caps, improbably large, don't you think? The herons gather here every year around the end of January, and their first business is to repair the old nests. When the trees are bare, they're easy to see. Look, there's one flying with a twig in is bill. Their feathers are smoky blue with darker streaks, like the fringe of a shawl. They'll repair their nests and then fighting for females will begin," I thought, going in my mind through the natural attractions of Stanley park in order to keep showing Laureano something interesting so he wouldn't suddenly disappear. "Canada Geese live over there by the pond. They've proliferated to such an extent that no one knows what to do about them. You can't kill and roast them for dinner. So what did they do? A terrible thing: remove the eggs from under the geese, give the eggs a vigorous shake, and put them back. The geese, suspecting nothing, continue to incubate the eggs. A park worker told me that, so, I don't know, it may not be true." My goodness, what rubbish! I suddenly realized, embarrassed by my own fantasies. And then something changed and I felt the cold on my back and grew depressed again as darkness fell.

I returned home with a sense of shame and regret.

5

Finding myself on Alberni Street again two weeks later, I felt a bit awkward and didn't know what to talk about. My teacherhimself suggested the subject.

"You know, I've always been interested in Russia. I even wrote a whole book about Lenin. But his grand experiment didn't work out. Tell me more about your life in Russia and the theatre in Omsk where you worked."

I couldn't conceal my astonishment—a book about Lenin?

"You never expected such a thing from me? Yes, for many years he was my idol. And not only mine. Everything progressive in our country and the rest of Latin America was inspired by his ideas. Lenin showed how to build a better, more just society. It wasn't his fault that mankind couldn't take advantage of his recipes."

I didn't know how to answer that. I had never taken any interest in politics, but even so I couldn't grasp how such an intelligent man could have been captivated by the ideology of a dictator responsible for the deaths of millions of people.

But Laureano no doubt spoke the truth, since the majority of Latin American leftists were confirmed Marxists. They admired the Soviet Union and accused the Americans of supporting and even instigating the many military coups on their continent. My own experience had convinced me of that. Thanks to Carlos, I had been accepted by the Latin American diaspora in Montréal. Its people were of the most varied kind and origin: Argentinians like Carlos, Chileans, Colombians, but they all seemed to agree on one thing: if the American imperialists had not grabbed all the natural resources and put dictators on the throne, there would be socialism, equality, and fraternity in their countries.

"Allende was my friend. If Pinochet hadn't seized power, Allende would still be alive."

"Was he a Communist?"

"He was the leader of the Socialist party, the Unidad Popular, but that isn't the point. He was one of those rare people who remain faithful to the ideals of their youth. And that required courage. He held onto those ideals in full measure. After Pinochet's coup a plane was put at Allende's disposal so he and his family could leave the country. But Allende make his own choice and shot himself. Much of what he had wanted to do he managed to achieve. He built schools and introduced free education for the poor. Have you ever been to Chile? Tens of thousands of its citizens were living in terrible poverty. Allende gave those people hope."

"Certainly, I understand. But tell me, it is true that you held a high position in Allende's government?"

The question was blunt, but Laureano answered it without evasion.

"I was a deputy minister of culture. When Pinochet came to power I had to leave.

6

After the fall of the socialist government in 1973, some 200,000 of Allende's supporters fled Chile. Could I argue about such things with someone who had lost his homeland and family, and who with that exile had secured not only his freedom but probably also his life? His friends and colleagues had been imprisoned and tortured by Pinochet's agents. Thousands more perished in concentration camps for political prisoners. The infamous Caravana de la Muerte, as the army officers given unlimited authority by Pinochet called themselves, tortured with exquisite sadism both imagined and real enemies of the regime who had already been sentenced to death. When the Caravana arranged public executions at the Santiago stadium, Laureano had already fled to southern Chile. Skirting Lake Maihue and crossing the mountains, he eventually reached Argentina and freedom. But Pinochet's secret service had a long reach. The car of General Carlos Prats, who had been a minister in Allende's government and commander-in-chief of the Chilean army, was blown up a year after the coup in the center of Buenos Aires, killing the general and his wife. Clearly, it was unsafe to remain in Argentina, and Laureano made his way to Mexico, as did many other Chilean refugees.

Laureano shared all that with me only in the most general way. The details I got later from Stella. And when in his hallway that day he was helping me on with my coat, holding it wide, I couldn't help asking,

"If you liked Lenin so much in theory, how cone you never went to the Soviet Union to see how it worked in practice?"

"Well, I can see that you're cross. I certainly didn't mean to offend you," Laureano said with a gentle smile. "You see, I'm an example of what people sometimes call a limousine liberal. But more seriously, I realized that your country would disappoint me, that I wouldn't find there what I had hoped to find, since Stalin had completely perverted Lenin's ideas. I'm sure that without Stalin, your country would have taken a completely different path."

7

It seemed to me after Laureano had shared some of the details of his biography that we might grow closer. But it didn't happen. At our next meeting he was aloof, even coldly formal.

"What shall we talk about? Something remote from politics?" he asked and then paused. "Well, all right," he said at last, "you still haven't told me very much about yourself ... Were you born in Omsk? Until you, I had never met anyone from Siberia, although I did have an acquaintance from Moscow. The only thing I know about Siberia is the enormous scale of nature there, its splendid evergreen forests, just like the ones here in western North America. The continents were connected at one time, you know."

"Yes, my grandfather took his life in those splendid forests," I thought, suddenly irritated again. I didn't care for my teacher's tone. It was as if he were quoting an advertising prospectus extolling the natural beauties of some exotic land.

"If I'm not mistaken, the Yenisei flows through Omsk, one of the longest rivers in the world ... We have beautiful rivers in Chile too, but they're comparatively short."

"Omsk is on the Irtysh, not the Yenisei. And the river's water was always a murky yellow. That's what I remember it from my childhood. Silty loam. I'm not really attached to the place, even though I was born there."

We fell silent for a moment.

"I may be old-fashioned," Laureano finally said, "and forgive me if it sounds trite, but a feeling of native rootedness, for the ground beneath one's feet, seems extraordinarily important to me for a person's sense of self. As long as that feeling exists, your can travel, or even live for a long time in foreign lands, without losing yourself. For our inner essence is to a large extent determined by our connection to the world into which we were born. The call of that homeland, sometimes powerful, sometimes barely heard, will sustain a person in difficult times, isn't that so?"

"Possibly. I don't know," I mumbled, staring at the fireplace. "Siberia has always been foreign to me, despite my having grown up there, maybe because our family had been exiled there. Had been violently expelled from our home and tossed into a cockroach nest! And then ... if they keep reminding you your whole life that you're aliens, then what kind of connection could there be? What kind of 'call'? But I think we agreed not to talk about politics."

Laureano came over to me and put his warm hand on my shoulder. I recoiled from the unexpectedness of it.

"Magda, you aren't cross with me, are you? Our conversation really was difficult last time, and it seemed to me then that I had offended you. Forgive me if I did. Believe me, it wasn't my intention at all ... Let's speak freely, just as we did before! And if it's disagreeable for you to recall your life in Siberia, then I ask you again to forgive me."

He smiled with just his eyes, charming me with their velvety affectionateness. At such moments its seemed to me that he could see into my soul like few others. I immediately relented.

"Oh, no, I wasn't offended ... I could tell you about it, only my family's story is a pretty ordinary one. Just like those of thousands of other people."

Not wanting Laureano to see my face, I stepped over to the window.

"My grandfather was a professor at the University of Lvov in what had been eastern Poland. Then, as you know, the Soviet Union and Germany partitioned the country, and the city became part of Soviet Ukraine. His wife and son - that is my father - were exiled to Siberia and my grandfather was sentenced to ten years in the camps. He felled trees in the camps just like everybody else...lots of Polish intellectuals were exiled and imprisoned. Somehow he managed to get two years off his sentence, and then when he was finally released and allowed to return to his family, they were all sent to a tiny settlement near Omsk and he couldn't bear it anymore and took his life. My father was five when they were sent into exile, and thirteen when my grandfather died. My mother was half-Polish and half-Ukrainian and she and her people had been exiled from Lvov too."

Laureano was now sitting in his armchair with his hand over his eye, as if he was suddenly very tired.

"Stalin's crimes rivaled Hitler's," he said in muffled voice. "That in fact was what I meant when you asked me why I hadn't visited the Soviet Union."

"But Stalin was sitting in the Kremlin, while my family was thousands of kilometers away in Siberia. Omsk still isn't anything, although it's considered a major center compared to Norilsk, say, or Dudinka. But that mercilessness didn't just come from Stalin, who had died in 1953. No, it came from the people themselves. It was in their blood—the envy, the cruelty. There's a Russian saying, you know, that it doesn't matter if my own eye is poked out, as long as my neighbor loses both of his."

Laureano gave me a quick glance and then looked away.

"Well, envy isn't only Russian—it's a universal human characteristic," he interjected while continuing to avoid my gaze. "Take that portrait of my son given to me by my friend, Gilberto. He was a talented and bold caricaturist. But political caricature as a genre was a potential threat to the regime, so when Pinochet came to power, my friend was arrested. Since I still had some connections, I tried to obtain his release. I acted through another artist, an old school friend of Pinochet's. The artist didn't have a scintilla of Gilberto's talent and was terribly envious of him. So he immediately said he couldn't help, although I knew that he had only to say a word and Gilberto would be freed. Then he started trying to convince me not to get involved, as if it would be dangerous to do so, and then when he saw that none of that had been of any avail, he started to openly undercut my efforts."

Laureano abruptly stood up and went over to the window. I could see that he was upset.

"I only meant that envy is the most widespread human quality. Marcus Aurelius said, 'When you wake up in the morning, tell yourself: the people I'll deal with will be meddling, ungrateful, arrogant, dishonest, jealous, and surly. They're like that because they can't tell good from evil. . .' But I say to myself, 'Today a miracle awaits me, for everything is possible in life, and none of it is foretold.'"

Laureano parted the curtains, letting somber January light into the room. A drizzle was falling, the cold, unpleasant kind so common in Vancouver in the winter.

"Look out the window. Even this grey day has its charm. The raindrops on the branches like crystal—is that really not a miracle? You know, during the junta, despite the terror, blood, and violence, people would risk their own lives to save their neighbors. Yes, that's right."

But had Laureano ultimately saved his friend, or hadn't he? I couldn't bring myself to ask.

He took a handkerchief from his pants pocket and patted his brow with it. The starched white triangle in his breast pocket remained undisturbed.

"Do you mind if I take off my jacket? It's getting hot in

here. Perhaps we should turn off the fireplace?"

He flicked a switch and the flame licked the pile of artificial logs one last time.

"Loving your neighbor, someone near at hand, is well known to be the most difficult thing," Laureano went on. "If the 'other' is completely unlike you, he might be tolerated, but if the difference is small, then atavistic laws of the cave take over. To root out that gene of rejection, people need to be trained, educated."

"In my opinion, education has nothing to do with it," I objected. "Those with a higher education often behave even worse than ordinary working people do. And you don't have to look very far for examples."

8

Whatever induced me to tell Laureano about the Omsk ballerina Shpalikova? I hadn't allowed myself to think about her for the longest time, but in Laureano's presence I softened. Something shifted in my soul and I ... well, I wanted Laureano to pity me. Remembering it now, I'm embarrassed by my candor. He could have suspected me of being craven or petty. Shpalikova was the company's prima ballerina, while I merely danced in the corps de ballet. Although a provincial company, the Omsk Dramatic Theatre was by no means the least among them. The population of the city was over a million, and directors and performers visited from capital cities. At the time we were staging *Esmeralda,* based on *The Hunchback of Notre Dame*. The great Bolshoi star Maya Plisetskaya happened to be visiting the theatre. She was asked whom she would recommend for the title role. The famous ballerina silently tipped her head in my direction. Naturally, the theatre's management was not pleased. Ballet is Russia's national pride, and the unknown Magdalena Tsevolskaya would suddenly be dancing the lead! It was the early 1980s, the years of Polish Solidarity when he position of people of Polish descent like me was even more precarious. But of course no one could dare argue with Plisetskaya. The dress rehearsal arrived. I was dancing the solo in the square in front of Notre Dame, when my legs suddenly gave way and I collapsed from sharp pain in my feet. Pain is something ballerinas are used to. Sprains and chronic foot sores are ordinary things, but this was different. I took off my toe shoes, removed the cotton padding in them, and found glass splinters in it. My toes were of course covered with blood. An investigation was begun, but as usual no guilty party was found, although they didn't look very hard either, and soon the business was dropped. When a month after I was able to dance again, the role of Esmeralda was no longer available. And then four years later as I was about to leave Siberia, Shpalikova (it was she of course who had danced *my* Esmeralda all those years) stopped me in the hallway and said, as if in passing, that she was the one who had sprinkled broken glass in my toe shoes. What made her confess? Certainly it wasn't remorse or a bad conscience. I asked if she wasn't afraid that I would report her. She opened her watery blue eyes wide in mock astonishment. "What do I have to be afraid of? Nobody would believe you anyway. But if you do take it into your head to complain, I'll deny everything." I understood then that she had had no other purpose in confessing than to humiliate me. She knew I was leaving the theatre and couldn't file a complaint, anyway.

My not wholly conscious calculation had been correct. Laureano took my story to heart.

He paced back and forth, puffing on his pipe, and then in an agitated voice he said, "What happened to you was terrible! That woman had no justification! But, if it's possible, you should try to forgive her. You can't judge a whole people by individual instances! For even among the most prejudiced, the most narrow-minded people, decent individuals will be found who will restore harmony. Obviously, to forgive an insult and especially an injustice is extremely hard, but it's the only way to make peace with yourself and thus with other people."

"Where had that Christian forgiveness come from?" I wondered in astonishment, since I regarded Marxism and Christianity as incompatible. In spite of myself, it provoked something insolent, even spiteful in me.

"And have you been able to forgive?" I said, almost blurting it out. "The death and torture of your friends, your own exile, have you forgiven that? Or are you still hoping for the restoration of communism, of a heaven on earth that will invariably lead to one and the same thing: torture and the destruction of life?"

I felt the blood rushing into my face and my palms
begin to sweat. But I got myself under control. Who was I to
teach him. To set him straight?

Laureano got out of his arm-chair, visibly agitated.

"Calm down, dear Magda! Don't be upset! You've had
a very difficult life and suffered a lot, and naturally ... "

"No, nothing of the sort!" I couldn't keep from
interrupting. "No, I've had a normal life! No particular
suffering at all! I've seen real suffering and I know what it is.
I saw the humiliation of the Poles in our settlement. And give
me the answer to this, explain the most terrible thing: why
some of them forgave their tormenters. And not only forgave
them but even justified them! That's what's incomprehensible.
'Chop down a forest and chips will fly!' they would say; that
is, since the Russians were building world communism, we
should suffer for that righteous cause! That's what's terrible!
Not ground glass in somebody's ballet slippers! That glass was
a trivial thing!"

I don't remember all that was said that day, but
somehow we made peace and in the future silently decided to
avoid the sharp corners.

9

In the mid 1980s around the time Gorbachev came to power,
my father's long-held dream of returning to Poland was at least

partially realized when he was allowed to move back to Lvov with his family. The people on my mother's side had remained there all along, although she had already passed away. The move was a lucky one for me. I was hired by the celebrated Lvov National Opera and Ballet Theatre. I remember my six years there as the best of my life. My father, however, still wanted to return to Poland, even though he was only five when the country's eastern part was absorbed by the Soviet Union. I think he wanted that return to his "real" homeland not so much for himself as for his father. I, however, was determined to live for myself and my own sake. In the end, he emigrated alone, and I remained behind with the theatre. My refusal to join him led to a complete break between us. In Poland, he had had to start all over again. He hardly even remembered the language anymore. He had been an outsider in Soviet Russia, and he would be an outsider in Poland too.

"You know," Laureano said after I had told him about my father, "I want to share it with you ... I too, finally have a chance to return home. Rosalia has been offered the post of cultural attaché at the embassy in Santiago. We were supposed to stay in Vancouver another year, but then that vacancy opened up. It's been twenty-five years since I've seen my homeland. We're planning to leave in April. I believe I can be of use to my country. What do you think?"

Laureano looked at me as if his fate somehow depended on my answer.

"What, in April? But that's next month ... " I blurted but

then quickly got hold of myself. "Of course, you'll be of use, of course you will. You've told me so much about Chile that I'd like to see it myself. You won't send me away if I should suddenly turn up to research an article about Santiago?"

"Well, obviously, obviously, come visit us. We'll always be happy to see you," Laureano quickly replied, and I understood that I was no longer of any concern to him.

10

Once mentioned, the theme of returning home never left us. Every conversation ultimately led to Laureano's departure and everything tied to it. It seemed to me that he felt guilty about his long, albeit enforced absence and was now hurrying to make up for it. He had one goal, to be of use to his fatherland, and he was already making plans for how he would do that.

During our last meetings, Laureano no longer sat in his armchair with his legs crossed while slowly smoking his pipe, but after greeting me remained standing or else anxiously paced from corner to corner. Sometimes he would take a book from its place on the shelf and then return it, as if considering whether or not to take it with him.

"Of course, there's a whole new generation now," he mused out loud. But he still had a few connections there! He had helped a lot of people in his day, some because of his position and its duties, and others out of friendship. And among his friends were professors, writers, lawyers and judges, movie directors, journalists. The children of those friends were now in the government and universities, so he wouldn't be forgotten! He grew more animated, and in the depths of his dark eyes brightly burned a flame I hadn't seen before. I agreed and kept nodding yes. I had at the beginning of our acquaintance unsuccessfully tried to lessen the distance between us, to become a friend and confidante. But mow that he was leaving, it seemed to me that I had at last achieved that goal. He was asking for my advice and sharing his hopes and plans as if I had become a family member and were packing my bags along with him.

A week before their departure, the Santalones gave a party. They were saying farewell to Canada, to their diplomatic colleagues and many friends, while Laureano was saying goodbye to his students.

Just before their departure the Santalones sold or gave away their own furniture. I got the small side table, the one on which Laureano had always put a silver tray with chilled drinks. Without the dark-blue tablecloth that reached down to the floor, it turned out to be an ordinary rattan thing from a cheap Indian import store.

11

Seven years passed. I often recalled Laureano, trying to picture his unknown life full of interesting encounters and important events in remote Santiago. It would to be nice to get a note

from him, however short, I would think. But I understood
perfectly well why there had been and would be no note.
First of all, I had during those years moved several times; and
second, who was I to him anyway? A chance acquaintance
at one of the numerous stops placed by fate along his exile's
path. But even so, even so, I thought, miracles do happen
in life. He himself had taught me to believe that. And never
having visited Chile even once, I could imagine the setting
any way I liked: majestic mountains with waterfalls, icy lakes,
and respectable cafés in the capital like the ones I had seen
in Vienna during the Lvov Ballet's visits there, with plush
upholstery, newspapers on wooden rods, large chandeliers,
and, moving among marble columns, attentive waiters in black
vests with snow-white napkins draped over their forearms.
Or Laureano shining with intellect and wit at diplomatic
receptions and easily eclipsing his boorish, ill-mannered wife;
or in a circle of writers and poets discussing the problems of
Chilean literature; or among political figures proposing a new
constitutional project; or speaking from a university dais with
hundreds of young eyes fixed on him. And, my goodness,
what a contrast to my own bland life and its daily routine!
Thousands of kilometers away here in Vancouver, I work as
a subcontractor on advertising brochures (something I had
been doing then for five years), while in the evenings I go to a
recreation club to teach ballet to ladies of retirement age!

Once, in early spring as I recall, I went for a walk in Stanley

Park. It was after a hard rain, and the park had a pungent, earthy smell, with still wet pine needles gleaming in the sun and the cedar trunks looking like velvet. Even the lichens hanging in pale grey tufts from the dead branches seemed to have perked up and taken on an almost greenish hue. The trees were covered with young foliage, and through it you could see, just as before, the fur caps of heron nests and rapier beaks on long necks, since the females were already hatching chicks, while the males hunted for food to bring back, standing with seemingly inexhaustible patience on one leg along the edge of the park lagoon.

I remembered the imaginary but never taken hike with Laureano to Stanley Park, and either from the fresh spring air or else because everything around was again young with the white rhododendrons already starting to bloom, it suddenly seemed possible for me to realize my dream. What was it? That I would buy a ticket and fly to Santiago and call him from the airport. "Do you remember me? The Eisenstein article, our English and Spanish lessons?" If Rosalia should answer, I would say I was there on a magazine assignment and in the city for only a few days, and that I wanted to take them both out to lunch if they could spare an hour or two.

When I got home, I called Stella to get the Santalones' address and number. She cautiously told me that Carlos had recently married. I hardly paid any attention to that news and immediately turned the conversation in the direction I needed.

"Yes, Laureano was indeed wonderful. My husband

and I miss him terribly," Stella chirped, glad to switch to a less fraught subject.

"Yes, it's so sad that he left. How times flies. It's been seven years, right? How has he been doing? Have you heard anything about him?" I said in a ordinary, everyday tone, suppressing a twinge of anxiety.

"Laureano died. Did you really not know?"

"That is ... Died how?! When?!"

"The way people do ... About three years ago."

"I ... I ... had no idea. Somehow I can't imagine that Laureano ... He wasn't that old."

"In his early seventies. An aggressive form of cancer. Enrico and I saw him about a year before he passed away. He was still healthy. We invited him out to a café and he was delighted. He complained about being alone and said that he spent whole days without exchanging a word with anyone."

"But how could that be? His wife was a diplomat and there must have been receptions and interesting people to meet ... "

"He and Rosalia had separated and Laureano had nowhere to go. His son took him in. His son, by the way, is an extremely successful doctor, but he didn't get along with his father because of something that had happened long ago. But when we saw Laureano—you remember what a dandy he was—well, we had invited him to a nice place and he, of all people, was wearing some filthy old worn-out old sweater. And the greedy way he ate especially struck me. He was obviously hungry. But then he cheered up and even joked and remembered Vancouver too and his old friends there. He asked about you and wondered if you had ever written ... "

"He asked about me? Thanks. That is ... What am I saying? But he really must have had lots of friends in Chile, lots of connections ... Or had the country changed so much in the twenty-five years he was away?"

"The country had changed, of course, but it wasn't that. A scandalous story came out. Only it's not to be passed on."

"There's nobody I could tell. Except for your brother, I don't know anybody you know."

"It was something that happened a long time ago when the junta seized power. An artist friend of his had been arrested, and while he was in prison, Laureano had an affair with his wife. Everybody knew about it, and when Laureano returned to Santiago, not only had the people of his generation never forgiven him, but he became a pariah, an untouchable."

So that's how it was, I thought after finally hanging up. So that's how it was ... Twenty-five years later and Laureano was a pariah, an untouchable! But what difference did it make now that he was gone? My face burned and my hands were ice cold. I couldn't bring myself to turn on the light. It was as if someone had slapped me, and in the dark it wasn't so painful or shameful. I opened the window and leaned against the frame. The fresh air helped. The Japanese plum trees planted in rows along both sides of the street were in the full glory of their ephemeral brilliance, and their dull wine-red leaves were barely distinguishable through the froth of the pale-pink bloom. The street lights had been turned on and their halos were pink. A subtle, sweetish fragrance filled the air. The central hospital wasn't far from my building. The sound of a siren cut through the air and the gentle fragrance of the blossoming trees: someone in an ambulance was in a race with death. I recalled my father saying that cancer settles—that's the word he used: "settles"—on those who suddenly find themselves with nothing to do, those whom life has pushed out of service. It washes them away like a wave, ridding life of unneeded ballast. That belief was firmly held by Siberian exiles.

"But how, how could his son have dared not to feed him? No, I'm going!" I suddenly yelled, shutting the window with a bang and running into the kitchen to splash my face with cold water. "I'm going to Chile to track down that Emilio and lay it all out as in a final reckoning." What would I say to him? That his father had been the most honorable and noblest of men! And what's more, a person of enormous charm! A source of light ... And in fact one of the few people in my life I had loved! No, there would have been no point in any of that; his son wouldn't have cared. The point wasn't love, but the precept that you have to forgive those close to you, and moreover ... But moreover what? That a son isn't his father's judge. But it wasn't his son who had judged him; it was Laureano's friends, it was life that had judged him. No, his son had judged him too!"

I couldn't fall asleep that night. An unknown woman kept appearing to me, the wife of the artist, and Laureano's exceptional love for her (that it was exceptional I had no doubt). I imagined his vain attempts to free his friend from prison. He must have tried doubly hard in order to escape temptation, but his love proved stronger than all the obstacles, stronger than the conventions of the world, than family, marriage, and ... the laws of honor.

It's true, I thought, staring into the darkness, it's true that their feeling was akin to one I had so many times been thrilled to conjure up on the stage, and with all the more conviction the less attainable it was in my own life.

By morning I had already begun to doze off, and in a half sleep I saw a theatre stage. In its lights two dancers were performing a *pas de deux*: Laureano was pleading with his beloved to share the fate of exile with him, while she, slipping from his embraces, was refusing to do so. Then onto the stage the young Emilio ran and rushed about looking for his vanished father. And as if someone had poked me in the chest I came to and sat up in the bed. A clear thought crashed like a cymbal in my head. There was nowhere for me to go. Laureano had passed away and long since ceased to suffer.

I heard the sound of a siren again.

The milky darkness of dawn was already creeping over the city.

Parting

1

"What kind is it?" Inga asked the enormously tall library patron as she handed him two Stephen Kings and a John le Carré.

"An African Grey," he said, smoothing the breast of the large parrot on his shoulder.

"Can it talk?"

"Say thank you, Pepa. Thank you for the books."

"Kiki, kiki," the parrot replied.

It was after that encounter that Inga at last decided to retire. And then, my goodness, she would finally be free to live her life the way she wanted! And instead of going to work at the library everyday as she'd been doing for the past twenty-five years, she too could get a parrot, say. The giant reader considered its intelligence superior to a dog's and even near that of a four-year-old child. Wonderful! Inga would teach hers to talk, and not just single words but whole sentences.

And after she and Arkasha (she already knew its name) had got used to each other, she would take up bonsai—cultivating dwarf pines or oaks in glazed ceramic pots. Then, and why not, she would enroll in a belly-dancing class. She wasn't the right age, of course, but it would still be good for her health, since with her high cholesterol and blood pressure she needed to lose weight. And then, and again why not, she could suddenly wave aloha to Hawaii! Only who would look after Arkasha? First the trip to Hawaii, then belly dancing, and then Arkasha and bonsai, in that order. Yes, except that she forgot the most important thing. Painting! She had for the last year completely neglected it. And people had been saying for a long time that she had talent. One expert had complimented her birds and insects in particular—she had a series of them—and compared them to Louise Bourgeois's spiders, even if she'd only seen Bourgeois in reproductions and hadn't liked them: severe graphics and a kind of scary geometry. And the French-American woman's last name was strange too. Was it her real one or did she make it up? No, Inga's acrylics were warm and lovely: gentle butterflies, domestic worker ants, tremulous dragonflies, affectionate titmice, wagtails, and finches. In general, her pictures were lively and sweet, and people bought them ... She had long wanted to switch from acrylic to oils, though leisure would be needed for that, since the technique was laborious and the paint took a long time to dry. "So, I'll work through the winter and spring, and next summer I'll retire, I'll certainly do it," she firmly resolved.

And then, after she had planned it all so well, that's when it happened.

It began with her mother asking her the same thing on the phone four or five times. That had put Inga on her guard, but she didn't really give it much thought, and stepping over the debris of repetitions as over things that had been accidentally dropped in her path, she went on with her life. During the day she handed out and sorted books, in the evening she got together with her girlfriends, people as lonely as she was, or watched TV serials, while every Sunday she did her washing and cleaning and cooking, and occasionally, if she had time, some painting and drawing. And only when a couple of weeks later her mother started to complain that people had been stealing her glasses, her keys, and now her gold wedding ring, it was only then that Inga gasped as if someone had just struck her in the solar plexus. "Just think!" mother said, "the ring with the little diamond that belonged to my grandmother shot by the Germans during the war—that they hadn't touched, and it's clear why. Diamonds won't mean anything to the rabble, but gold, well that's something else!" But Inga didn't panic that time either. She quickly covered over in her mind the flaw that was beginning to look like a precipice, put on her sandals, and set off for the drugstore as she meant to do, since she needed to get some vitamin B3, which was supposed to be good for her arthritis.

However, when her mother called her one morning at work to tell her that the entire human race without exception consisted of gangsters out to poison her, the sheet of paper Inga had just taken from the printer started to dance in her hands as she thought in terror of the cruel duplicity of fate that instead of her beloved, clever, beautiful mother was trying to pass off that.

To get a grip on herself that evening after work, Inga took down from the shelf one of her mother's books. Her mother was considered one of the best translators into Russian of English and Italian poetry and had continued to translate even after becoming the editor-in-chief of a large Moscow publisher. Interspersed in the little volume of Cavalcanti canzones Inga was holding with her mother's preface, translations, and commentary were reproductions of works by Giotto, a contemporary of the poet. Looking at the pictures she remembered her and her mother's last visit to Italy fifteen years before. In Padua they had "dashed" into the Scrovegni Chapel to see the Giotto frescoes, since visitors were allotted only fifteen minutes. They were taken past throngs of saints with golden haloes and narrow, Chinese slits for eyes, and Inga's mother, straining to be heard above the constant hum of the dehumidifier, said that Giotto had departed from the dominant Byzantine style with the invention of a unique optical illusion—an early example of Renaissance perspective. Her mother stopped in front of the fresco depicting Judas's kiss, and Inga kept staring at it, trying to see what it was that had struck her mother. Judas's was a crude Neanderthal-like face with a low brow and projecting jaw. He was rudely thrusting his jaw towards Jesus's face for the treacherous kiss that would serve as the signal for his teacher's arrest. But Jesus was looking at Judas with a tranquil firmness without moving his face away him.

"Did he really betray him for money? He was his disciple, he loved him ... Was it the usual greed? Or maybe envy of his teacher's fame?" Inga wondered when they were back outside.

Her mother squinted in the sunshine and inhaled the gentle, perfumed air with evident pleasure.

"How lovely! Can you smell it? Either acacia or blossoming oleander. Just wonderful!"

Inga's mother could take exquisite pleasure in the smallest things: from sunny weather, or a new little scarf, or a glass of fine wine. Inga never could yield to trivial things that way, could never let herself go over trifles. It was as if there were a tightly wound coil inside her that she could release only when she was painting her wagtails.

But her mother was free. Instantly changing registers, she could turn from a delighted girl into a scholarly adept able to discourse on "celestial topics," as Inga called them. Her mother's intellect was acute, her erudition and memory were immense, and Inga had known from childhood that there was no one like her.

"Greed, you say?" her mother picked up the conversation begun outside the Scrovegni. But I, for example, don't think it could have been anything so insignificant. I have no doubt that Judas loved his teacher. One theory says that an everlasting plan was being fulfilled through Judas. If he hadn't betrayed Jesus Christ, there would have been no crucifixion, and mankind would not have been saved. Christ knew, after all, that one of his disciples would betray him, but he couldn't oppose the will of God. Which is why he's so composed in Giotto's rendering. Actually, Borges refuted that idea in his "Three Versions of Judas," as you know, right? Or is there no

177

call for him at your library?"

"Mama, when would I have time to read? A shoeless cobbler ... "

"Well, obviously, you don't have time," her mother scoffed, "which is why I'm telling you. So Borges, or the character of his little sketch, thinks that Judas wouldn't have had to single out Jesus with a kiss. Everybody already knew who he was. He had openly preached, healed the sick, and performed miracles. No, the reason was a more subtle one. By the way, did you notice how Judas was dressed? In a bright-yellow, golden robe that was almost the same color as Christ's halo; that is, Giotto had depicted him as a reflection of divine energy as it was interpreted by theologians and painters after them. Christ shares his spirit with the traitor, with his betrayer."

Inga's mother tossed back her dark chestnut hair with its grey streaks, raising her face to catch the warm breeze. They stood still for a moment, unsure of where to go next. Two young men glanced at them and then continued to look at her mother. Inga was used to the fact that it was her mother who attracted the attention of men, even though she was shorter than Inga was and twenty-five years older. There was something about her that was lacking in her daughter: an abundant joie de vivre that was apparent in every gesture, in her smile, in the turn of her head, and most of all in her lively, laughing dark-blue eyes.

"To me, it seems that Giotto just wanted to put Judas in the center of the composition, and that's why he chose the bright-yellow toga ... So he would stand out," Inga said.

"Well, he could have clothed him in red, the color of blood, and you wouldn't have failed to notice that either. But instead we have noble gold. That is, the heavenly, the exalted, and the earthbound have at a certain point come into contact with the mean and base. And at that point the opposition of their natures disappears. Read "Three Versions of Judas" yourself; it's all there. How is it in Borges? Judas is one of the twelve apostles, he's been singled out, acknowledged, and it follows that he's entitled not to have his motives interpreted in such a primitive way. He's a mirror image of Christ. Christ chose a base death by crucifixion. Judas chose death by eternal dishonor. It's as if he considered himself unworthy of goodness. His treachery was an extreme form of asceticism and abnegation."

"How could that be? It turns everything on its head," Inga muttered, starting to lose the thread and growing distracted. The University of Padua was nearby. Crowds of students were hurrying about among its columns.

In the rarified atmosphere of speculative constructions Inga's mother was in her element, and Inga could keep pace in thought neither with her, nor all the more with Borges, and quickly lost interest in the abstract discussion.

They found a little café with an ivy entwined courtyard, and Inga, who was fond of sweets, ordered tiramisu, while her mother sipped a cappuccino through a plastic straw.

Her mother avoided deserts on principle: she was watching her figure. Taking hold of the back of her chair, tipping her beautiful head back, and youthfully crossing her legs, exposing her plump, nylon-clad knees without any of the boniness of age, she examined the other customers with interest.

"Look, they're the same faces we saw in Giotto. The young woman over there at the corner table—see? - with her broad peasant face like his Madonnas. You close your eyes and it's as if seven centuries had never passed."

Inga's mother took a notebook from her purse and jotted something in it. As long as Inga could remember, her mother had always been writing things down: an unexpected thought that had just occurred to her, or a word that she'd been looking for. It didn't matter where she was. She wrote things down in the subway, while driving, while having supper with her family, even in the presence of guests. But this time when she took out her notebook, her eyes, undimmed by age, impishly lit up under the thin arches of her raised eyebrows. "You know, Giotto had a lovely sense of humor. Once as he was walking down the street, there was a herd of swine coming the other way. He wasn't alone, of course, but accompanied by friends - in those days people rarely went out alone. The streets were muddy, and the swine splattered Giotto with mud as they went by. But he didn't take offense! He was eternally in their debt, he said, for there was no telling how many of their bristles had gone into making him brushes."

Inga closed the copy of Calvalcanti. It was already

around midnight and she needed to get up early the next morning. She took a sleeping draft, which would leave a bitter taste in her mouth the whole following day, but still couldn't sleep. The horror of what lay before them drove sleep away. Staring into the darkness, she kept remembering her mother the way she had known her all the long years: amiable, quick, and successful at whatever she did.

2

Inga's father died when she was four. Her mother raised her, with her grandmother sometimes coming to Moscow from Leningrad. Then Inga got married and left with her husband and children for Toronto. Her mother didn't want to give up her beloved work, and so for a time she remained behind in Russia. It was never said in so many words, but it was understood that the separation was temporary, that sooner or later mother and daughter would be reunited some other place on the globe. A few months after their arrival in Canada, Inga's husband fell in love with a clerk at a Russian store and left her. Fearing further unpleasantness (they all knew each other in the Russian community), Inga left with her children for Vancouver. As a single parent she needed help, and it was then that her mother finally decided to join them. And just as it had been in Inga's own childhood, so it was now: home was wherever her mother was. The magical gift of taking a strange place and turning it into a comfortable home delighted Inga, since it was a gift that she had never possessed.

And there was in Inga's mother, besides her strong will and clear, sharp mind, something that drew people to her, making her the center of any situation: merriness but especially an inner resolve that inspired the certainty that that diminutive, blue-eyed woman with a quick smile that lit up her whole face could find a way out of any situation, and that everything around her would somehow work out, and work out, moreover, in the best possible way. Her mother was an unerringly accurate judge of people and could anticipate what they would do, and Inga, as indecisive as her father supposedly was, had like all their relatives and acquaintances grown used to relying on her mother's advice.

Diffident by nature herself, Inga was amazed by her mother's fearlessness. Mother had been afraid neither of the KGB generals who kept a close watch on her publishing house, nor of the Minister of Internal Affairs of Georgia, a protégé of the Stalin's henchman Beria, who after noticing her on a beach at Pitsunda on the Black Sea coast of Abkhazia when she was still a young woman, pursued her for a long time. He would come to Moscow and arrange to meet her in fancy restaurants. To put an end to the business, Inga's mother, without a word to anyone, packed a small bag and vanished from Moscow for two months. Where she had gone not even her husband knew.

Sober pragmatism was combined in Inga's mother with an inner zeal, even an excess of empathy. Unhesitatingly, like a sailor to a gun port, she rushed to the aid of any sufferer. She commiserated, she phoned, she hurried across the city, she cajoled, she nagged. And knowing the irrepressibility of her own nature, she sometimes masked her inner fervor with irony or with an intentional aloofness or even brusqueness.

Inga was the epicenter on which the vectors of her mother's love converged. As an adolescent Inga had been confused. The magnetic field of that maternal love was so powerful that for a long time she could not decide just who and what she really was. However, with the years Inga not only got used, but even made herself at home in that citadel that provided such a secure defense against everyday tempests. And just as it would be impossible to live without air, so it now seemed absolutely impossible to Inga to live without the abiding gift of that passionate, energetic, maternal interest in her, without their mutual concern and sympathy.

How, why could that powerful and, it seemed, inexhaustible spring have begun to dry up? How could it have happened that the hand the already greying Inga had got so used to feeling in her own over the long decades was now inexorably slipping away? How, why had her mother suddenly left her, even if Inga herself was no longer young and starting to fade but still forever needing her? To put it right, to prevent it, to return everything to its previous place—that thought tormented Inga, even though she knew that she could not avert the catastrophe, that it was inevitable. She shivered and gasped for air as if there weren't enough oxygen and busied herself, starting first one thing and then another, but lacking the strength to finish any of it.

Once in September as she was coming home from work later than usual and a hard, cold, relentless rain was falling, and it was so dark all around that she could barely see anything at all, Inga let her tears stream under the cover of the darkness and then began to wail like a simple Russian village woman, and all the more since no one could hear it in the car. "I won't survive this catastrophe, please, take it away, stop it, I won't be able to handle it, I haven't got the strength, I won't get through it, I just can't!" she pleaded to God in whom she had never believed. And suddenly off to the side of the road and high up in the air in that pitch-dark wetness, a fiery cross appeared that seemed to hang in the sky all by itself. Only afterward did Inga realize that she had been driving past a Catholic church, its steeple topped by an iron cross with lights along its edges. But at the time that cross appearing out of nowhere struck her as a frightening portent, as the pointing finger of God, as a crucifixion, only not Christ's but her own. This is your cross, this is your Golgotha.

3

Inga brought her mother groceries, cooked and left meals for her, and did the cleaning. And she drove her to look at the "puppies" too, a new pastime in which her mother took squealing delight. As they neared the dog park, her mother would stick her head out the window and, ignoring the pet owners, start yelling, "Here boy, here boy, come to me, silly, let me kiss your little mug! And that other stupid one, get out of here! Go away! It's written all over your face that you're a dummy!"

They had been in Canada for twenty-five years, but when they went to restaurants Inga's mother would now, without a trace of doubt, address the servers in Russian, since her English had largely evaporated, along with a good portion of her other three working languages. Her whole professional life had been directed to bringing in all its fullness and clarity the thought of one person to the consciousness of another, but now she was completely indifferent to the fact that she wasn't understood. "They're just pretending!" she would exclaim. "I'm explaining it all very clearly to them!"

And sometimes her mother would ramble on without stopping about panty hose or a banana she'd eaten that morning, while Inga in keeping with a recently acquired habit would absently nod. But once, as if scalded, Inga caught out of the corner of her eye that her mother was tearing the chicken apart with her hands and then licking her fingers. Inga winced inside and started coughing.

"What's wrong? What's the matter with you?" her mother immediately reacted.

"I got a bone stuck in my throat," Inga lied.

"Why are you eating bones? Here, take my chicken. Take it and eat it, I'm telling you!" and her mother pushed her plate toward her.

After that supper in the restaurant, Inga returned home
exhausted with her head ringing like a bell. And now as she
recalled the moment, she broke into a sweat, just as he had
done then. She threw off the covers and sat on the bed in her
nightie. Pressing her hands between her knees, she suddenly
started to rock from side to side. That metronomic movement
calmed her. The collapse of logical connections in her mother's
mind partly resembled a return to childhood, or removing
articles of clothing: first her memory, then civilized habits.
And how unreliably flimsy was that clothing, how easily it fell
away!

Inga sat listening to the swish of tires on the street
outside her window. A siren howled and then the sound faded,
dissolving into the night. It was stuffy in the room. The moon
gazed through the open blinds with bright, indifferent face. And
Inga, hardly moving her bloodless lips, began to explain to that
silent interlocutor that it was out of pity, out of love for her,
that her mother had contrived the long, gradual crossing into
nonbeing.

So Inga would have time to get used to her absence.

4

A year passed before Inga finally took her mother to see a
geriatric psychiatrist, and the doctor, a tall, tanned, handsome
man with an ingratiating smile, leaned back in his chair,
stretched out his long legs in their patent leather ankle boots,

drew a circle on a piece of paper, and asked her mother to put numbers inside it with arrows showing, say, a quarter after six.

"If you want, you can check it against the one on the wall," he said with a friendly glance at the clock behind her. Inga's mother turned the paper one way or another and then suddenly burst out laughing. It was evidently amusing to her that the doctor had given her such a trivial assignment. What did he really take her for? Could it be that she appealed to him in a womanly way and he was flirting with her?

"If you think about it, who needs a watch these days?" she exclaimed, slapping her palm on the desk and merrily pushing the pencil and paper away. "Young people will soon completely forget what a clock face is. They have only, what is it, well ... those watches that light up with numbers," she started to mutter in Russian.

"You mean digital watches? Or cell phones?" Inga prompted.

"Exactly right!" the doctor animatedly replied. "Clock faces will soon fall out of use. Which is a pity, isn't? I, for example, am used to my watch. It tells me the month and the year too. Now it's August. Can you name the months in reverse order? August, July, and so on?"

"Do it in Russian, Mama, and I'll translate," Inga said.

"Why? I can tell him in English. Doctor, I can't stand August! The heat, and midges or something. There never were any before. It's an awful time, August, isn't it!" she exclaimed, not realizing that she was answering in Russian. Inga looked down and translated.

"Very good," the doctor said without reacting to the inappropriateness of the tirade. "Can you try to name five words that begin with F?"

"It's unlikely she would be able to in English," Inga quietly observed, turning toward the doctor so her mother wouldn't hear.

"That doesn't matter, whatever is easier for Mrs. Ol-Ol-khovsky. You'll translate for me."

"Fifa! They called me a fifa in school because I wore a hat with a veil!" Inga's mother said, using an old slang term for a tart and breaking into loud laughter with a coquettish gesture.

Inga hesitated, unsure of how to respond.

"Fifa is an old expression, doctor. Perhaps she could recall something else? Mama, can you remember any other words that begin with F? Maybe Friday or something?"

"I already told him! Enough of him!" her mother said indignantly.

Inga blushed, embarrassed by her mother's abrupt, completely unmotivated change of mood. The doctor noticed it and, as it seemed to Inga, said in an unbefitting, falsely hearty tone, "Well, excellent, Mrs. Ol-olkhovsky! Very good, indeed!" and then turned to his computer and rapidly typed something on the keyboard.

At that point Inga took a folded sheet of paper from her purse, opened it, and quietly pushed it across the desk to the doctor. Written on it were two words: dementia and

Alzheimer's with a question mark following each word. Distracted from his computer, the doctor glanced at the paper out of the corner of his eye and then quickly drew a circle around the word Alzheimer's.

"Sometimes it's hard to differentiate, but the picture here is clear enough. An early stage," he added, looking up at Inga.

"How many in all?" she asked in a lowered voice.

"Stages? Usually seven, but that doesn't mean ... "

"I understand, I understand, and how long does each one last?"

"Again, that depends on the individual. The first, from three to five years; the second, it's hard to say. In all, that is, from the initial diagnosis to ... In a word, perhaps as much as ten years. But I repeat, it's hard to predict anything."

The doctor turned back to his computer screen.

"When did you first notice that your mother's memory was failing?"

"Over a year ago."

"That's usually how it goes. Even two years may pass between the first symptoms and a visit to us. And in general the process of memory loss can begin even earlier, sometimes as much as a decade."

"He's going on about memory as if there were nothing more to it?" Inga thought in vexation. "My mother is no more! Her personality's gone, but for him it's memory, memory!"

"You know," Inga quickly said in a low voice while

leaning over the desk toward the doctor, "my mother was very smart, someone of great erudition. That is, not was, but is. She has a doctorate and is a gifted poet, and I just don't understand how such a thing could ... Naturally, nobody's immune, but with her intellect I expected whatever you like, only not this. No, that isn't what I meant, forgive me, I know it's silly, but all the same I just cannot ... I just cannot ... Perhaps there's some medication?" Inga concluded, aware that she could no longer control the muscles in her face, which was about to contort in an indecent tearful grimace.

"I completely understand. I'll prescribe some vitamins for her. They'll halt the process temporarily. And improve her memory," the doctor hastened to reassure her.

"Is there anything besides the tablets that might help?"

"It can be beneficial to go out everyday, to take a walk."

Inga realized that her mother was doomed.

She started to feel faint, as if the air had suddenly been pumped out of the office. Why
didn't she let herself go, why didn't she reveal the extent of her despair? But it seemed to her
then that that impressive and by all appearances successful person would not really be able to grasp the full horror of the catastrophe that had befallen them. Although Inga understood with her mind that the doctor was in no way at fault, it didn't help. For him, as she saw it, her mother was just a patient, another file with a disease history among hundreds of other files, whereas their situation was unique, although not as a

disease, no, but because her mother wasn't like anyone else ... "Those creases in his pants, razor sharp. Who do you suppose irons them for him every morning? His wife? A housemaid?" Inga thought to herself with disgust.

She was drowning, and the only one who could have thrown her a lifeline was her mother, but her mother was herself departing into unknown depths and not even aware of it. The doctor was about to write out a prescription when there was a knock on the door. A young blond woman of unprepossessing appearance came in.

"Sorry I'm late. There's construction everywhere and the roads were closed."

"Come in, come in ... We're just about finished here."

The doctor indicated a chair with a tilt of his head.

"This is Neshka Boleznova who's interning with us. You won't mind? By the way, she's a former neighbor of yours—from Bulgaria."

He handed Neshka some papers and lowering his voice quickly added, "Take a look. High IQ patients can sometimes use their intellectual capacities to compensate for other deficits."

"What kind of name is that, Boleznova?!" Inga wondered with distaste as she examined the intern's shoes: lettuce-green ballet slippers with little multicolored seashells on the tips.

"Maybe you could prescribe the same vitamins for me too? Some tablets, perhaps? Something strange has been happening with my own memory," Inga said, masking her despair with a playful tone.

The doctor stared intently at her and then slowly said, "Those tablets won't help you."

"No? But why not? I'm not so young myself. Sometimes a word will be on the tip of my tongue but I can't think of it!"

"Those tablets will only help with Alzheimer memory loss. Temporarily, " the doctor repeated in the same flat tone.

"But what's the difference?" Inga said, refusing to yield.

"The difference is that you're aware of what's happening to you, while Alzheimer patients aren't. But keep in mind that memory is often worse under stress, as is typically the case with people who look after the sick. You're close to your mother, are you not? In such situations there's often a transference, an identification with the person who's dear to us. We may subconsciously mimic or project his illness onto ourselves."

Here he confidingly leaned toward Inga.

"You need to take a break at every opportunity. And find your mother a home for ... people with that disease. If you need documentation, I can help."

"What? Already?"

"You unquestionably need to plan ahead. She won't be able to live very much longer by herself. A crisis typical of the disease will eventually occur and you need to be ready for it."

5

Outside it was sweltering. There had been no rain all summer. Everything seemed to gleam in a special muted way. You wanted to hide from it, but there was no escaping: the diffuse sunlight followed, surrounding and exhausting you.

"Why are you so upset?" Inga's mother wondered as they got in the car. She had unerringly caught Inga's mood, just as she had always been able to.

"They gave us a bad diagnosis, Mama."

"What diagnosis is that? That I'm crazy? Who cares what he said! Don't believe doctors. They're only good for filling out forms."

"No, she still doesn't understand," Inga thought in despair. "She doesn't understand any of it, just as he said ... "

Inga had no close friends, although she did have acquaintances. "You and your mama were buddies, right? Think how lucky you were! I can't stand the sight of my mother," one of them said. "Oh!" Inga said thinking of something else. She was gripped by another fear: that she would remember her mother the way she was now, with the image of her decline eclipsing that of the woman who had once been gifted with talent, beauty and rare vivacity.

Another acquaintance said, "Would cancer have been better? At least your mother isn't suffering physically, so be thankful for that." – "I'm very thankful," Inga replied and made a point of never contacting that friend again.

Losing your reason in plain view of everyone. Of all the possible sentences, that's the most terrifying, she thought. Yes, and who said she doesn't suffer? Staggering through a murky forest of dwindling consciousness, her mother would still stumble on sunlit patches, on untouched glades of light. And then would recoil in horror from the inexorably approaching darkness.

In one of her lucid moments she said, "It's like wading into the sea without returning, and you just keep going, keep moving forward without a backward glance. But I am a coward. Help me. Help me do it."

The hardest thing for Inga was her mother's phone monologues. She spoke excitedly, vehemently, as if under siege. The trivial actions of her neighbors seemed like deliberate crimes. While her indignant voice went around and around, Inga, putting the phone down on the kitchen table, would wash the dishes, put everything away, and even sweep the floor. Coming to the end of a sentence, her mother would invariably return to its beginning, and it was astonishing that despite its loss of content, her speech retained its precise grammatical structure. Like learning a foreign language, only in reverse, Inga thought. When the lexical stock is limited, you get by with general phrases, you step around and adjacent to your own thought, simplifying and distorting it. Or else it's like when you're flying and you look out the window and see only the general outlines of the city you're approaching, but then as the plane is landing, you can make out buildings and little toy-like cars speeding along the highways. Whereas with her mother it was the opposite: the higher she climbed, the denser the fog that obscured the details of the landscape and left in her field of view a limited assortment of demonstrative pronouns: "So it's that, that thing, that what's it called? That, you know."

Inga's mother took care of herself the way she had always done. She plucked the little hairs on her chin, touched up her eyebrows with a dark pencil, trimmed her fingernails herself. But the more she "maintained her form," the more Inga recoiled from it, though not so much from her mother's frailty as from the erosion of her consciousness, from the illogic of the speech that in Inga's youth had intimidated her with its meticulousness, its irrefutable arguments, and the richness of its phrasing. Something about that revulsion was instinctive, as if Inga were afraid of infection.

She had learned from pamphlets that Alzheimer patients have a special need for affection, but that very affectionateness, that simple physical contact, was something Inga avoided. The loss of memory had brought with it a loss of personality, and without personality there is no life. To hug a shell in which death was hiding meant to yield to death yourself.

Inga reproached herself for that. After all, is the essence of life really in logical thought, in intellectual activity? Plants and animals don't discuss things. Her mother still experienced taste, smells, color, hot and cold, delicious and not delicious, pain and not pain. Even though life had narrowed the eye of the needle, it was still life. Or wasn't it? Her mother still played the piano and had recently finished a biography of the poet Joseph Brodsky, even if she couldn't recount a single word of it. Life or not life?

And for the umpteenth time Inga sworn to be gentler, kinder, more patient.

Her mother gave off a heavy, ineradicable odor of old age. And despite Inga's promises to herself, she would try to shorten her visits.

But when the mother was hospitalized with double pneumonia, Inga pleaded with all her heart to some invisible being to let it pass, for her mother to survive.

6

To get to the hospital, Inga needed to drive across the city. At first in front the windshield flashed residential blocks with one- and two-story wooden houses behind cypress, yew, Japanese holly, and boxwood hedges. The crowns of mighty chestnuts, maples, and elms met overhead in continuous arches, with the long, slender, rain-laden seedpods of broad-leafed catalpa sometimes lightly sketched between. There would be gaps in that luxurious foliage, since many residential blocks were slated for destruction. It seemed in fact that a war was going in them, that they were under siege and bombs were randomly falling first on stately Victorian mansions, then on the gingerbread roofs of Tudor cottages. Inga had changed cities

many times in her life, but a city bent on subtracting itself
street by street from her space without her moving from her
spot had never happened to her before.

The houses fated to be bulldozed could be identified
at a distance by orange plastic netting stretched over
rectangular wooden frames to screen certain trees from the
new construction sites. It was said that a million new residents
would soon be moving to the city. Orange rectangles were
added daily. As Inga drove past, on the left and right flashed
ditches and pits surrounded by piles of dark-brown dirt and
gravel, and then rippling orange netting again. According to the
papers, in one year alone some 1,500 residential buildings had
been razed, although Inga thought the figure underestimated
the true number. It was known that Chinese millionaires were
buying up the land, and that the greedy city authorities were
doing nothing to preserve the local architectural styles. The lots
were subdivided, and where once there had stood a spacious
home with a garden, three houses without gardens sprang up,
the original lawn paved with asphalt. Since quality played no
part, they built with lightning speed. Often what was built was
larger and uglier than what had been torn down.

As Inga proceeded east, the residential blocks gave
way to a commercial zone. There the denuded land was packed
with mirror-black cubes and truncated tetrahedrons housing
computer firms, insurance companies and real estate offices..
The lots between the structures were filled with rows of new
and used cars for sale, their windshields competing to catch

the soccer ball of the August sun. To lure buyers, little flags of various colors were stuck along the perimeters of the lots, and sometimes waving in the air above was a tethered figure made of what looked like large inflated sausages. From the air pumped into the creature, it came to life like Frankenstein and waved its lopped-off sausage arms, and there was something indecent about the way it would suddenly double over from a gust of wind as if it had been punched in the stomach.

Inga's mother did survive but was very weak, and when she regain consciousness she was unsure of where she was and said that the nurses had been secretly dealing drugs the night before. She begged to go home.

Once after feeding and calming her mother, Inga stepped out into the hospital hallway for a breather and noticed a young man in a wheelchair by the nurses' station. He devoured her with his eyes the way no man had looked at her in twenty years. Either he was attracted by the festive summer dress that clung to her plump but still pleasing figure and so paid no attention to her face, or else in the hospital's absence of real fish her crayfish had been enough for him. She blushed and lowered her eyes. And in lowering them she realized that he had stumps for legs. They had been amputated above the knee.

The legless young man was young, a bit over thirty, probably. He had a sort of egg-shaped head that may have looked that way because it was shaved. His face, however, was full, without creases or the pallor of people who've spent much of their time in hospitals. It looked like his misfortune was fresh and he still hadn't gotten used to it, still hadn't lost the habits of a healthy person, which is very likely why he had looked at her so greedily.

7

The way home lay due west, and in the haze the setting sun blindingly shimmered along the upper edge of the windshield. Holding onto the steering wheel with her left hand, Inga rummaged in the glove compartment for her sunglasses, but they were no help. The diffused light breaking through the thickening milky-grey haze beat against her eyes and temples. There were no clouds to be seen, but the now yellow-grey haze had become so thick that she had to turn on her headlights, which produced strangely indistinct shadows. In a corner of the windshield and seemingly just outside it glimmered something round and bright: the blood-red disk of the sun. Amazingly, she could look directly at it without squinting. She had never seen anything like it. It wasn't a solar eclipse but something else, something unaccountably disturbing.

Slowing down, Inga continued west. Mixed with her usual post-hospital fatigue there was now a feeling of vague regret. About what? - She wasn't quite sure. That legless young man, she had shrunk from his gaze and averted her eyes as if frightened by his deformity, that's what it was. People don't want to create burdens for themselves and instinctively look

away, and she too had lost heart and acted like everyone else...
But how should one look at the mutilated? By pretending
they're no different than anyone else? But that would be a
sham, a deliberate lie. With a person who has lost his legs, a
catastrophe has occurred, the everyday details of which healthy
people cannot even imagine. To look with sympathy, with
compassion? Would that not be humiliating for the person
who's deformed?

But isn't there a shared humanity that unites us over
and above our physical conditions, over and above injuries and
amputated legs? Yes, without legs it does unite us, whereas
without memory it may not. Without memory there's no being.

That night for some reason Inga dreamed about the legless
man, although his features were blurred, with other features
she had not recalled for years beginning to show through them
as in an old film. An invisible director has shifted something,
had altered the dream's decor, and now she was at a girlfriend's
dacha outside Moscow long ago in the month of May. She
was dreaming of a meadow, every bit of it down the last blade
of grass lit up by the sun and fragrant with the warm, bitter
smell of wormwood, cornflowers, and chamomile; and in the
dream she was again permeated with the affectionateness and
openness to the world that are experienced only in very early
youth.

Air of a deep, gentle blueness seemed to stream with
bliss, and the day was enhanced and given voice by the

presence in the dacha next door of a youth with wide-set eyes of a quiet, deer-like dreaminess. He was tall and slender, and when he leaned over her, his straight, rust-colored hair fell across his forehead. He pushed it back with his hand, and for some reason the gesture seemed special and was remembered. Inga's head spun from the nearness of his calmly pensive light-green eyes. From happiness and timidity she began to laugh: a grasshopper had jumped onto the hem of her calico dress, and that seemed funny; and the grass tickled her bare heels, which was a source of mirth too. But the main thing was that the deer-like youth liked her, and it filled her whole being with intoxicating joy.

In front ran two hounds, temporarily entrusted to them by an aging ballerina, another neighbor (since the dachas were for the artistic elite), and Inga and Seryozha (as he was called) pretended to be English aristocrats hunting hares. And then, gripping the dogs tight by their collars, Seryozha asked, "Shall I call out a hare for you?" and suddenly started to bay like a hound (Inga hadn't at all expected that he could make such loud, harsh sounds). From the woods nearby a white hare jumped out, and the tip of its tail was black, as if it had been dipped in ink—that she saw clearly and remembered. The hare stood erect on its hind legs and then instantly disappeared beyond the edge of the woods.

Inga and Seryozha met again in Moscow the following winter. Fluffy, freshly fallen snow limned the tree branches, doubling their size. The buildings looked like gingerbread. It was calm and soothingly festive. Without touching each other, they glided along the sparkling black surface of the icy runs formed on the sidewalks, as if trying to prolong the bliss of *that summer* day, but they were sixteen, no longer kids, and the childish skating seemed awkward and contrived. A handful of fluffy snow fell off a branch down Inga's collar. Seryozha silently watched as she took off and shook out her fur coat, and she remembered how detachedly he watched without offering to help, remembered because it was then that she, stamping her feet and shivering from the cold, understood that their holiday had ended. Why it had she no longer remembered and perhaps she didn't even know then.

That summer day, the happiest of her life, remained the only one, never to be repeated.

Seryozha with the deer-like eyes became a famous writer, and Inga, a dyed blond putting on weight and suffering from arthritis and varicose veins. The years lived through since were as grey as mice, and none stood out from the rest. Her life had for the most part consisted of overcoming hardships: two divorces and between them a desert of loneliness, dull years of work in libraries, a daughter and son from different marriages who had no time for her, and now her mother's illness.

Inga started to feel sorry for herself. She ate a thick slice of chocolate cake with white frosting as she always did when she was tired or upset about something. Then it was time to go to the hospital. She put some plums in a bag for her mother and thought she would treat the cripple to some too as a way of doing something nice for him. Plums are good for the digestion. But how to offer them? "Hello, I got them for my mother and have some left over?" No, that wouldn't work. She would have to come up with something but didn't want to think about it just then and decided to rely instead on the circumstances.

She saw the legless man from behind as he was going down the hallway, energetically turning the wheels of his chair. Then he turned around and came back toward her just as fast. Apparently, the motion amused him.

"I've got some extra plums. Would you like them?" Inga said with a tentative smile as the young man was abreast of her. He stopped and indifferently ran his eyes over her as if he'd never seen her before. She felt the strap of her camisole slipping off her shoulder, which embarrassed her even more, but she didn't try to straighten it.

"What would I want plums for?"

"My mother's in the next room and I'm taking her some. But she doesn't eat that much, and so I thought ... Well, maybe your relatives don't come very often, so why don't you take them instead? Plums are good for the stom ... "

Inga cut herself off mid-word: it all sounded wrong somehow. The young man was wearing a tee shirt that exposed his tattoo-covered biceps: two clenched fists on one arm and a three-eyed owl on the other. The front of the tee shirt read, Zombies eat brains. You're safe!

"If you're so full of compassion, why don't you go get some beer? Maybe the cafeteria has it. Though probably not. And what would my relatives be doing here? I haven't got any."

"Nobody at all?"

"Well, there are two boys: one in seventh grade and the other in fifth. They would be considered relatives, yes. Only they don't visit. They're scared of seeing their legless dad. Or maybe their mother won't let them come ... "

"Excuse me, it's obviously none of my business, but doesn't your wife visit?"

"She used to be my wife, but we split."

Inga looked at his stubs and immediately averted her eyes, just as she had the first day. But he noticed her glance.

"No, it was before that. When I was alive and healthy. I was a soccer coach at a school and coached my own kids too. I wanted them to be stars and everything was going really well for them. Someone from an elite US program came to see me and said he would take both of them, since they were talented kids."

He was silent for a moment.

"So I'd just bought a house and was making a real effort for my wife. And while I was doing all that, she left me for some Greek guy. Got custody of the kinds," he said, looking down at his stumps.

"What you're saying is terrible!"

"What's terrible about it? It's life!" he said defiantly.

"Even so, you mustn't lose hope! The children will grow up and understand and come back to their father. I'm waiting too ... waiting for my son ... trying not to lose hope, since everything changes."

"It does? Well, that's obvious enough. But I don't care any more. I made an effort for my kids. And what did I get for it? A smack in the head."

He turned abruptly and quickly wheeled himself away without taking the plums.

Inga continued to her mother's room. Her mother was muttering something, and Inga drew the curtain that separated her mother from the patient in the room's other bed, sat down beside her mother, and then couldn't stand it anymore and burst into sobs. Her mother stopped mumbling and reached out her hand to her.

"What's the matter, my girl? Is it because of me?" Inga smelled the hospital air, a mixture of disinfectant and camphor.

"I'm sorry, it's just that my nerves are shot. But you're better, they saved you, and that's the main thing and all I need."

"What's upsetting you then? That I keep repeating things all the time? That I forget words? But how old am I, after all? Well, yes, I'm finding it harder to think clearly, I say stupid things sometimes, but I'm still alive! And I love you as much as I ever did. When I'm truly dead and gone, then you can cry. But for now you really must not, my little one, you must not be upset about me. I've lived a very long life. And it wasn't designed for that."

"What wasn't, Mom?"

"My body wasn't designed for such a long life. It happened by accident. But so far we are still alive! And will continue to be for a while longer! You remember how it is in that poem?

"Which poem, Mama?"

"Why, in the one, what's it called?"

"Whose?"

"I translated a lot of him. He drank and died young. During a reading tour in America. He was from Wales ... "

"Do you mean Dylan Thomas?"

"Yes, yes, that's the one ... He has a ... a poem about the sovereignty of death. It's the famous ... wait a second, I'll remember : 'And death shall have no dominion ... ' It goes, 'Under the windings of the sea,/ they lying long shall not die windingly' ... And before that, 'Dead men naked they shall be ... ' And something like, 'When their bones are picked clean and the clean bones gone,/ They shall have stars at elbow and foot;/ Though they go mad they shall be sane,/ Though they sink through the sea they shall rise again.' That's all I can remember. It means that those who are losing their reason will recover it. That those who have drowned will be raised up. Death shall have no dominion ... Go home, my child. And don't come tomorrow. Take care of yourself. You've been through enough as it is.

It was already starting to get dark when Inga left the

hospital. There was a burning smell in the air, and the yellow-grey haze now covered the whole city as if it had sunk to the bottom of the ocean. You couldn't see more than five meters in any direction. It was with difficulty that she even found her car. On the radio they said that forest fires had surrounded the city in a tight ring and that over 200,000 acres of forest had already burned. She finally got home and unlocked her front door.

Her porch railings were coated with a fine layer of ash. There was ash on the window ledges and the tree branches too. She turned to look behind. In the ash covering the porch she had left a narrow trail of footprint.

About the Author

Marina Sonkina is a Canadian fiction writer, journalist, and educator. She is the author of *Expulsion and Other Stories, Tractorina's Travels, Runic Alphabet, Lucia's Eyes and Other Stories,* and *Stalin's Baby Tooth,* as well as of several books for children. Her recent experiences as a volunteer in a refugee camp in Poland are recounted in *Ukrainian Portraits: Diaries from the Border.* A novel, *Larissa,* is forthcoming.

Marina Sonkina lives in Vancouver, and on the Sunshine Caost, BC.

Printed in the USA
CPSIA information can be obtained
at www.ICGtesting.com
JSHW072036220224
57846JS00016B/154

9 780995 277823